PSYCHIC ZONE
CHANGELINGS

The Psychic Zone

THE
PSYCHIC
ZONE

CHANGELINGS

MATHEW STONE

Hodder
Children's
Books

a division of Hodder Headline plc

A Catalogue record for this book is available from
the British Library

ISBN 0 340 69840 3

Typeset by Avon Dataset Ltd, Bidford-on-Avon, Warks

Printed and bound in Great Britain by
Clays Ltd, St Ives plc

Hodder Children's Books
A Division of Hodder Headline plc
338 Euston Road
London NW1 3BH

CONTENTS

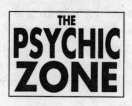

THE PSYCHIC ZONE

Prologue

Invitation to the Feast

Dateline: Trans-Plutonian Space;
5000BC.

It was only eight hundred million kilometres away now, the closest it would ever get – for now at least. In astronomical terms that was nothing. A mere blip in the unimaginable vastness of interplanetary and inter-stellar space. The craft and its pilots had travelled much further than that in their ages-long quest throughout the outer reaches of the galaxy. A galaxy which, one day in the far-off future, would be known by some as the Milky Way.

For a single half-instant the craft paused. It hung in the blackness like a mote caught in a sunbeam; like a spider waiting in its web.

If there had been thinking creatures to watch – and, of course, there weren't – they would have described the ship as a blazing ball of light, with a long white tail of flame trailing behind it. It was similar to many of the comets and meteors which circled this area of space.

But the ball of light was much more than that.

This wasn't the first time that the ball of light had visited this part of the galaxy. The last occasion had been just over seven thousand years ago. Then the creatures on board the ship had been disappointed with what they had found.

Disappointed, but not sad. Not annoyed. That would have been a waste of valuable emotions.

But no matter. The creatures were infinitely patient, if nothing else. Seven thousand years ago they had discovered nothing to excite them. This time it might be different.

There were planets circling the medium-sized yellow star, on to whose co-ordinates the ball of light had locked. The creatures reached out their minds to those nine worlds: checking; evaluating; researching. Looking for food.

The first, outermost planet they came to was cold and sterile. Covered with a sheet of frozen methane. Silent and dead. Nothing to feed on there, the watchers decided.

The next four planets were equally unpromising. Large, ringed, gas giants. Surfaces constantly ravaged by untamed storms. Poisonous atmospheres.

Nothing there.

The next world further in seemed a little more hopeful – for a few moments. The watchers were quickly disappointed: the red planet had once supported life, but now it was dry and dead. Apart from a few basic bacteria, of course, imprisoned in the rocky soil. Hardly enough to sustain life.

So, no food there either. Was their mission doomed to failure?

And then the watchers started chittering excitedly to themselves. Emotion swept throughout the ball of light, before the passengers checked themselves. They quietened down and looked much more calmly at the planet: the third one out from its sun.

Could it be? Had they finally found what they were looking for? And on such a small and insignificant world as well!

The last time the watchers had turned their scanners on to the tiny blue planet it had seemed that they had met with failure again. True, life had developed down there in the planet's oceans. True, creatures had learnt how to leave the waters, learnt how to walk upright on dry land. But those creatures possessed little intelligence apart from a few basic skills. By the goddess, they had only just come down from the trees! They were not what the watchers needed.

Maybe in a few million years, they had said. Maybe then life would have developed enough for their purposes. That was what the watchers had thought. But they hadn't had that much time.

That was seven thousand years ago. And how much

life had developed in those seven thousand years! Much faster than anywhere else in the galaxy, much faster even than the Talking Plants of Esto! Here was rich food indeed!

But how could they be sure? They had to check much more closely. If they were wrong then thousands of years would be wasted. They couldn't afford to lose any time.

A small pinprick of light detached itself from the main craft: a survey ship. Crewed by the bare minimum that could be spared.

Then the mothership sped off into the darkness of space. It would return when its task was nearly complete. It would return in seven thousand years to see if the mission had been a success.

The smaller craft paused for one final half-instant. Then it headed off on its journey to the small blue planet.

A small blue planet that would one day be known as the Earth . . .

THE PSYCHIC ZONE

1

Darkfell Ring

Dateline: The Darkfell Rise;
Monday 1 June; 13.15.

'Man, like this is going to be the greatest rock concert in the entire history of greatest rock concerts. And you know something? I can't wait!'

Rebecca looked superiorly at the black New York kid who was dressed in the sort of hip-hop streetwise clothes she'd only ever seen before in MTV videos. 'Joey, they're just another band,' she told him.

There was sheer disbelief in Joey Williams' eyes, and he looked at Rebecca as if she were mad. Or past it, he reconsidered.

At fifteen, Rebecca might be only a couple of years older than him, but sometimes she behaved as though she were in her twenties, with a place reserved at the nearest twilight home for the terminally uncool. Take her clothes, for one thing. Sensible black top and designer jeans which she'd ironed this morning. Ironed, for Chrissake! Only Rebecca Storm ever ironed jeans!

'Just another band?' he said. 'That's like saying New York is nothing more than just another little hick town. Or that the Institute is just another village school.'

'Or that Momma Leona's Sun-Dried Triple Blue Cheese with Pepperoni and Avocado is just another takeaway pizza,' put in Marc, who, when he wasn't studying at the Institute, was usually thinking about his stomach.

'Zarathustra are like the most crucial, most happening band of the past twenty years!' said Joey.

Rebecca smiled indulgently and then threw back her head, enjoying on her face the warmth of the June sun, which shone in her long auburn hair. She, Joey and Marc were enjoying a picnic on the Darkfell Rise, that grassy hill which overlooked the Brentmouth Institute for Scientifically Gifted Youngsters. At least, she and Marc had been enjoying the picnic. Joey had been doing nothing else but going on about his favourite rock band for the past twenty minutes.

'They've also been disbanded for fifteen years,' she reminded him. 'Two years before you were born.'

'That's the whole point, Bec,' said Marc, who shared Joey's enthusiasm. 'This is going to be their big reunion concert, out here on the Rise.'

'Yeah,' said Rebecca, singularly unimpressed. 'A bunch of talentless forty-somethings making clowns out of themselves. Like I'm interested!'

'Maybe you're not, but several hundreds of

6

thousands are,' Marc reminded her. 'Pretty soon now, this place is going to be the scene of one of the wildest open-air gigs in years. Bigger than Reading, the Fléadh and Glastonbury put together!'

Rebecca shuddered at the thought, picturing the crowds that would be converging on Brentmouth village. Although she wasn't a fan of the band, she knew that Joey was right. Zarathustra had an enormous following, from the forty-somethings who had been their original fans, right down to kids like Joey who hadn't even been born when they'd played their farewell gig. There was a tangible feeling of excitement in the air. Some of the students at the Institute had been talking of nothing else for weeks now, and the school noticeboards had been covered with posters of the band.

'I'm surprised it's being allowed at all: there's lots of local opposition to it. General Axford is dead-set against it, for one,' she said.

'The final say-so hasn't come through yet, but it will,' Joey said with cast-iron certainty. 'I mean, which mean-thinkin' over-thirty could deny any sentient being the right to see the best-loved rock band in the history of the universe?'

'Anyone who isn't tone-deaf,' Rebecca said, and Joey gave her a friendly punch in the ribs. The kid from the New York slums had been getting on very well with Rebecca since he'd arrived here in England on a mathematics scholarship, and he knew that she was only teasing him.

'*And* the local folklore society,' added Marc.

'Ah yes, our friendly neighbourhood weirdos,' Rebecca remarked. 'What's their objection then?'

'They're scared that all the people coming to the gig will vandalise their precious stones!' he said. 'According to them, the stones are built on sacred land.'

Rebecca shaded her green eyes from the light of the sun and looked down the hill, past a copse of trees, at the Darkfell Ring. Some said that the old stone circle had been there since the beginning of time.

Rebecca didn't believe that, of course. She'd read a recent archaeological survey which dated the stones at only six or seven thousand years old. Still, that did make them a couple of thousand years older than Stonehenge, which even she had to admit made the Ring slightly interesting.

With its six standing stones (compared to Stonehenge's twenty-plus), the circle wasn't as famous as its counterpart on Salisbury Plain. Nevertheless, every year tourists still came to walk the hills and wonder at the megaliths.

Some said that the six standing stones possessed deep mystical powers. Others believed that they were six evil-doers who had been turned to stone by a witches' coven. Still others said that the stones could somehow reach deeper into the universe than even the radio telescope on nearby Fetch Hill.

As far as Rebecca was concerned, they were just a pile of old rocks. 'The folklore society are welcome to them,' she said. 'I can't imagine anyone being interested in something like that.'

'Bec, you've no soul, no sense of romance,' Marc said despairingly.

'I'm a scientist, Marc. Just as you and Joey are. I'm not interested in the past. It's the future that concerns me.'

Marc pulled a face at her. She was being too serious for her own good, he told her, and Rebecca had to admit, with a smile, that maybe he was right.

'Yeah, chill out, Rebecca,' Joey advised her. 'Let's just lie back in the sun and enjoy our day off school. No boring lectures. No General Axford breathing down our necks telling us we should be studying in the library. No homework.'

'*I've* still got my astronomy assignment to finish,' Rebecca said. 'I should be working on that and not wasting my time out here!'

Marc groaned and handed her a can of Diet Coke. 'Rebecca Storm, one day you are going to be the best scientist the Institute has ever produced, or –'

'Yes?'

'Or the biggest bore on the face of this planet!' he said.

'Pig!' Rebecca laughed and was about to pour part of her drink over him when they heard a buzzing sound and then a weird sort of *put-put-put* noise approaching them. She looked up into the cloudless sky. A small plane was flying through the blue, leaving a white vapour trail in its wake. It looked so peaceful up there, she thought.

'It must be heading for the airfield,' Marc said.

'Airfield? What airfield?' Joey wanted to know.

'It's a military base they sometimes use for civilian flights when Luton's not available,' Rebecca told him.

She sat up and squinted to see the plane better. She'd once travelled from London with her mom in a tiny five-seater, and she knew that the plane had begun its descent much too soon.

'Guys, I think there's something wrong,' she said urgently. The craft started to spiral out of control.

'It's going to crash!' Joey realised. He leapt to his feet, shading his eyes from the sun.

'Can't the pilot do anything?' Marc asked.

'It's too late!' Rebecca realised. She watched on in horror as the plane passed out of sight behind the trees.

'Come on!' Marc urged. He was already racing down the hillside towards the scene of the crash. 'It's gone down near the Darkfell Ring. We have to go and help!'

**THE
PSYCHIC
ZONE**

2

The White Witch

*Dateline: The Darkfell Rise;
Monday 1 June; 13.43.*

The light aircraft spotted by Marc, Rebecca and Joey
had, in fact, crashed quite a way off from the Darkfell
Ring. It took them about fifteen minutes to reach the
site. The plane's descent had been broken by the trees,
and the wreckage wasn't quite as bad as they had
feared. At least the engine hadn't exploded, which had
been Rebecca's worry. Still, the fuselage was twisted
and torn, one of the wings had been ripped off, and
there was a gaping hole in the starboard-side. The
plane's belly had been battered and buckled beyond
recognition. There was a worrying smell of petrol in
the air, Rebecca noticed.

'Careful, Marc,' Rebecca said as he approached the
plane and heaved himself up on to the starboard

wing. 'It might blow up at any second.'

'If it was going to it'd've done it by now,' Joey said and followed Marc. Rebecca realised that Joey was probably right, and joined the two boys.

Marc had already clambered along the wing of the plane. He was heading towards the cockpit window, which had been blasted open in the crash.

'We have to see if we can help the passengers,' he grunted, pulling himself along. 'They'll be trapped under the wreckage.'

Rebecca looked uncertainly at the wrecked plane.

'Shouldn't we wait until the emergency services arrive?' she asked.

'We've no guarantee that they're on their way,' Marc said. 'Remember it's a bank holiday today. Half the village have packed up and made for the coast, or gone down to the smoke. We could be the only ones who have seen the plane crash.'

Still, Rebecca thought it very unlikely that anyone could have survived the crash, and told Marc so. Marc ignored her and peered in through the cockpit's smashed window. And then he gasped.

'It's not possible!' he said.

'What's up, pal?' asked Joey. 'Something wrong?'

Marc remained looking through the smashed window for a few more seconds. Then he turned back to Joey and Rebecca. There was a very worried look on his face.

'I think both of you had better take a look inside,' he said. He pulled first Joey, and then Rebecca, up to see.

'I don't believe it . . .' Rebecca gasped once she had taken a look. 'The plane's empty!'

'Then the passengers must have survived the crash and dragged themselves out of the wreckage,' Joey guessed. Rebecca shook her head.

'There's no way anyone could have crawled out of that.'

She drew his attention to the bent and broken fuselage. Part of it lay across the pilot's seat, which would have prevented his escape. The fuselage at the back of the plane was so contorted that anyone sitting there would have been crushed to death. 'You'd have to be Houdini to get out of that.'

'That's crazy.' Joey took another look inside, as if to confirm the evidence of his own eyes. 'A plane can't just fly by itself.'

'It's impossible,' Rebecca agreed. She joined Marc, who had jumped down to the ground.

Before Joey did the same he spotted something lying on the pilot's seat. He brushed away the splintered glass and reached for it. It was an envelope, with a distinctive crest at the top left-hand corner. As he walked over to the others, he ripped it open.

Rebecca turned to Marc. 'What could have happened to the passengers?'

'Maybe they just vanished into thin air?'

'What do you mean?'

'Beam me up, Scotty,' he said and grinned mischievously. Rebecca groaned.

'I should have known better than to ask someone who keeps watching endless re-runs of *Star Trek*! You seriously think that they were teleported away by someone or something? That's impossible!'

'Tell that to the crew of the *Mary Celeste*. Or anyone who's flown into the Bermuda Triangle.'

'And you're saying that this plane is some kind of airborne *Mary Celeste*? Get real, Marc. Either that, or get your head seen to!'

'It would explain what's happened to the passengers though, wouldn't it?' Marc said. He started to walk away from the wreck.

Joey followed. He'd opened the letter now and was reading its contents with growing excitement.

'Listen, guys, we know who two of the missing passengers were,' he said and handed Marc the letter.

'We do?' Rebecca asked. She nodded over to the letter which Marc was now reading. 'What is it?'

'It's a letter confirming their enrolment,' Marc said and passed it over to Rebecca. 'For the Institute.'

'The Institute?' Rebecca gasped. 'Two of the passengers were down to attend the Institute?'

'I spotted the envelope on the pilot's seat,' Joey said. 'I recognised the school's crest.'

Rebecca speed-read the form. 'Romulus and Remus Hawthorne,' she read out their names. 'Cute.'

'You ever heard of them?'

'No way,' Rebecca replied. 'But if they're new kids, I'd imagine that the only people who'd know about them would be the General.'

'And Eva, of course,' Joey reminded her. 'Ever since the General had that accident earlier this year, Eva's been handling all new admissions to the Institute.'

So involved were they in their discussion, that none of them heard the footsteps approaching them from behind.

'Plane crashed, has it?' the voice said. They all jumped with surprise. The voice was deep and booming but still recognisably female. 'You won't find any bodies of course.'

They all turned round to see a stout and formidable woman in her early sixties looking past them towards the crashed plane. She was dressed in a checked hacking jacket with matching deerstalker hat, a tweed skirt and sensible shoes, and she was leaning on a gnarled walking stick. A pair of *pince-nez* spectacles were perched precariously on the end of her nose, seemingly defying all the known laws of gravity.

'Miss Rumford,' Marc said, recognising the president of the local folklore society. He'd once had reason to ask her advice on an anthropology paper he was working on, and ever since then the old lady had taken something of a shine to him.

Miss Olive Elizabeth Rumford was the sort of lady of a certain age who could be found in any English village. She had been born and lived in the same house as her parents, and their parents before them. Very much her own woman, she had never married (gossip spoke of a sad love affair a long time ago). Many people made fun of Olive Rumford; but no one could actually bring themselves to dislike her.

'What do you mean, you won't find any bodies?' Rebecca asked, after Marc had introduced her and Joey to the old lady.

' 'Course you won't,' Miss Rumford said. 'They didn't last time, did they? Or the time before. And they won't this time either.'

'Last time?' asked Joey. 'Like planes are always getting wasted around here?'

Miss Rumford winced at Joey's strong Harlem accent and his use of slang. Nevertheless she continued, addressing most of her remarks to Marc – who at least spoke with a proper English accent, even though she really wished he'd wash all that bleach out of his spiky hair.

'Back in the eighties another aircraft crashed just a few miles away,' she told them. 'They couldn't find any corpses then either, even though they looked hard enough. Practically dug up the entire Rise, they did. Same thing happened in the early nineties as well.'

'*They*?' Marc was really interested now.

Miss Rumford shrugged her broad shoulders. 'The Government? The Mafia? The BBC? Who knows?' she said. 'Men in black suits and dark glasses. With weird-looking scientific contraptions anyway. Caused no end of trouble to the Ramblers' Association. We liked to walk over the Darkfell Rise, y'see, but then the Men in Suits cordoned off the area.'

Marc, Rebecca and Joey exchanged excited looks. They had all heard of an organisation known only as the Project. One of their number had even kidnapped Joey before he had enrolled at the Institute. No one quite knew who the Project were, or even who they were working for. What they did know however, was that they seemed to be more than casually interested in the goings-on at the Institute and its surroundings.

'There's been trouble around here for hundreds of years now, of course,' Miss Rumford continued. 'Thousands of years, some say.'

'Trouble?' asked Rebecca. 'What kind of trouble?'

'Mysterious disappearances.'

'You mean, *abductions*?' said Marc.

'Abductions, disappearances, call 'em what you like,' Miss Rumford continued. 'Ever since records began. People spirited off to heaven knows where and never seen again. Like Seth . . .'

'Seth?' asked Rebecca and wondered why Miss Rumford had hung her head sadly.

'It doesn't matter,' Miss Rumford said and regained her usual composure. 'Or if they did come back, then they were . . . well, changed in some way. . .'

'Changed . . .' Marc's ever-fertile imagination began to think of a thousand and one reasons for the mysterious abductions.

Rebecca glared at him. She knew that he'd come up with a perfectly ludicrous reason for something which in the end would turn out to have a completely rational explanation. Already Marc's mind was full of theories of monstrous aliens kidnapping people in their flying saucers and taking them off to planets light years away.

'You hear that, Bec? Listen to what Miss Rumford's saying. She talks good sense.'

'But why did all those other people get zilched around here?' Joey asked.

'Zilched?' Miss Rumford asked. She despaired of the future of the English language and made a mental note to present the Institute library with a copy of *The King's English*.

Marc smiled. 'Joey means "disappeared", Miss Rumford,' he explained.

'Obvious, isn't it?' she said, and pointed to the Darkfell Ring. 'It's all to do with the stone circle.'

Marc's face brightened up again at the mention of the Darkfell Ring, while Rebecca raised her eyes heavenwards and sighed. Miss Rumford really had no right to fill Marc's head with so much rubbish.

'No one knows quite who built it or what for,' she said, warming to her subject. 'Some say it was a temple to the ancient sun god. Or to the devil.'

Rebecca groaned again.

'Others say that it was built to predict solar eclipses . . .'

Rebecca smiled. Now that seemed perfectly rational. That she could believe in.

'But there's certainly mystery in those stones,' Olive Rumford continued. 'Something magical.' And then she shuddered. 'Or perhaps something evil.'

'Evil?' scoffed Rebecca. 'How can you know that?'

Miss Rumford stared at Rebecca as if she'd just asked how she knew that two and two made four.

'I'm a witch, that's why,' she said, as if it were the most normal thing in the world. 'White, of course. There's always been one of us in the Rumford family for hundreds of years now. Passed down from one daughter to another.'

Rebecca tried hard not to snigger. 'Seventh child of a seventh child? That sort of thing?'

'Yes,' Miss Rumford said in all seriousness. 'I feel things more than other people . . .'

Rebecca raised her eyes heavenwards once more. As far as she was concerned, Miss Olive Rumford was a lost cause.

'Didn't I read that there are these dimbos who have cosy little get-togethers around the stones about the time of the summer solstice?' Joey asked. He immediately wished he hadn't: Miss Rumford fixed him with a steely stare.

'Some of those "dimbos" are friends of mine, young man,' she said sharply, putting Joey very firmly in his place. 'They have celebrated the solstice since before anyone can remember. And whatever you may think of their beliefs, you can't deny that the presence of so many worshippers must have filled the stones with some sort of psychic energies.'

'Psychic energies?' Joey was interested now.

'Of course. All ancient places of worship possess some magical properties,' Miss Rumford said casually, as though it were the most normal thing in the world. 'Westminster Abbey and Chartres Cathedral. Stonehenge and the Darkfell Ring. I imagine that's why the Old Ones chose the Ring as their home here in Brentmouth.'

'The Old Ones?'

Rebecca and Joey had no idea what Miss Rumford was talking about now. Marc, however, did. He started fervently to wish that the old woman would shut up.

'Why, those who are too evil for Heaven and too holy for Hell, of course,' Olive Rumford said in a matter-of-fact voice. 'The *Túatha de Danaan*, the Green Folk, the Elder Race, the Little People.'

'Er, Miss Rumford, I think that me, Bec and Joey really ought to be going now,' Marc said awkwardly. 'We ought to tell someone about this plane crash, y'know . . .'

'Wait a minute, Marc,' Rebecca said, with a gleeful grin on her face. She turned back to Miss Rumford. 'What exactly do you mean?'

Olive Rumford sighed. 'The fairies, of course! The fairy folk who live within the Darkfell Ring!' she said. 'They're the ones who've been responsible for the recent burglaries here in Brentmouth, I've no doubt. And they're the ones who have spirited away your precious passengers and everyone else who's gone missing down the centuries as well. They've been stolen by the fairies, my boy, that's what's happened!'

And with that, Olive Rumford, white witch, stumped off down the hill. *What do the youth of today learn up at that fancy Institute of theirs?* she wondered.

Rebecca and Joey turned to Marc, who was looking distinctly ill-at-ease with himself. In fact, his whole face was now puce with embarrassment. If the ground had opened up beneath his feet at this precise moment he would have been enormously grateful.

'Well, well, well, Marc Price,' Rebecca said sarcastically. 'So Miss Rumford knows what she's talking about, does she?'

'Hey, that's not the point, you guys,' he said. 'The point is that people really have been disappearing in or around the Darkfell Ring for centuries now.'

'Not "disappeared", buddy,' Joey said, joining in with Rebecca's good-natured teasing. ' "Kidnapped" was the word she used.'

'And not just snatched by any old gang of kidnappers,' Rebecca continued. 'So tell us, Marc –'

'Tell you what, Bec?'

Rebecca looked at Joey. 'What do you think, Joey? Should I ask him, or should you?'

'You ask him,' Joey decided, trying hard not to laugh. 'He's less likely to punch you in the face!'

'OK, Marc,' Rebecca giggled. 'Tell us the truth now. Do you really believe in fairies?'

THE PSYCHIC ZONE

3

The Needle's Eye

Dateline: The Darkfell Ring;
Monday 1 June; 14.12.

'Come on, you lot, give us a break!' Marc pleaded, once Rebecca and Joey's hysterical laughter had died down.

'Why should we?' Rebecca laughed. 'You were right on Miss Rumford's side, when you thought she might have been talking about aliens abducting all those people!'

'But when she said that she was talking about fairies!' Joey chuckled. 'Oh man, did you ever change your tune then!'

'So you tell me what the Darkfell Ring's for then,' Marc said grumpily.

'Not as the site for fairy balls, that's for sure!'

'It was probably used to predict solar eclipses, just

like she said,' Rebecca decided, after she'd had another good laugh at Marc's expense.

'And why do you think that?'

'Well, that's what Stonehenge was used for,' she said. 'Of course, I've got no proof. I'd have to take a look at the stones to be sure.'

'So let's do it now.'

Rebecca looked at her Swatch. 'Marc, we really ought to tell Sergeant Ashby down at the police station about the crash.'

'There's no hurry. No one's been hurt.'

'Sure they haven't,' Joey laughed. 'The fairies have whisked them away. They're probably looking after their injuries in the pixies' general hospital even as we speak!'

'Just shut it, will you!'

'We've also arranged to meet Colette later,' Rebecca reminded him. 'At least she'll love all your talk about fairies and old legends.'

'I want to show you two something,' Marc said, clearly annoyed at Rebecca and Joey's good-natured teasing. 'To prove that some things aren't quite as straightforward as you would like to believe.'

Marc's tone was so serious that Rebecca and Joey agreed to accompany him on the five-minute walk down to Darkfell Ring.

When they arrived there, Joey shuddered.

'What's wrong, Joey?' Rebecca asked.

Joey shrugged his shoulders. 'I don't know. I've been living at the Institute for a couple of months now, but I've never been here before. It feels kinda ... kinda ... spooky ...'

Rebecca sniggered. 'Not you as well, Joey! Don't worry – you're only tuning in to the fairies!'

She looked at the six stones which formed the Darkfell Ring. Despite their name, the megaliths didn't, in fact, form a circle. Instead they made a rough kind of equilateral triangle.

A small stone stump, only a metre high, formed the apex of the triangle. Situated roughly seven metres away, two much larger stones made up the other two angles. These stones were leaning sharply in opposite directions, one out to the left, one to the right. Midway along the base of the triangle there was another large stone. Finally, in the exact middle of the triangle there lay a large horizontal slab and a thin tall stone, two metres high. At the top of this stone someone had long ago bored a small hole. The earth within the triangle was barren, although outside it the grass was lush and green.

'It reminds me of something,' Rebecca said as Marc led the way into the centre of the Darkfell Ring.

'Reminds you of what?' Joey asked.

'I don't know. That's what's worrying me.'

By now all three of them were standing in the middle of the circle and Marc indicated first of all the central slab.

'Some people reckon that this was probably the main altar stone,' he told Rebecca and Joey. 'Where sacrifices were made to the sun god.'

'Or the fairies,' Rebecca teased. She placed her hand on the slab. It felt warm to the touch. It had probably soaked up the heat of the sun, she thought.

The slab was covered with strange inscriptions which had been carved into the hard rock. Rebecca wondered what they meant. If they meant anything at all, of course, she told herself sternly. For all she knew they could just be a series of dots and lines joined up together. Still, they vaguely reminded her of obscure mathematical symbols and she asked Joey if he recognised any of them.

'Sorry, guys,' he said. 'I might be majoring in math but goblin geometry ain't my bag.'

Marc glared evilly at him. Joey guessed that he'd gone too far this time, and he raised his hands in an appeasing gesture. 'OK, Marc. Just joking, big buddy, just joking. Carry on.'

Marc pointed to the tall stone with the hole at its top. 'That's called the Needle Stone,' he told them. 'The hole, they call the Needle's Eye.'

Rebecca walked up to the stone and peered through the Eye. In the distance she was able to see the buildings of the Institute. Further off, she could just make out Fetch Hill, and the saucer shape of the radio telescope perched on top of it.

'They probably observed the sun through this,' Rebecca assumed. 'When it was immediately in the centre of the Eye, I bet it meant that it was time for the poor so-and-so on the altar stone to get the chop.'

'Yeah, that would be the logical thing to assume, wouldn't it?'

Was it Rebecca's imagination or was there the faint suggestion of a sneer in Marc's voice?

'Of course, it's logical. I always am,' she said and

couldn't resist adding: 'Unlike some people I could mention.'

'There's only one problem with your theory, Bec,' he said. Now there was no mistaking the mocking tone in Marc's voice.

'And that is?'

'The sun rises in the east and sets in the west. So why does the Needle's Eye look to the north?'

Rebecca could have kicked herself. Of course Marc was right. She should have spotted that herself.

'Well, perhaps it was built to observe the phases of the moon instead,' she suggested weakly.

'Or maybe it was meant for some other purpose.'

'Does it really matter what these Stone Age guys got up to?' Joey asked impatiently. 'Whatever it was, it's not as if we're ever gonna find out, is it?'

'I guess not,' Marc admitted.

'So let's get out of here then.'

Joey was much more sensitive than either Marc or Rebecca and there was something about this place that made him uneasy. It caused the hairs on the back of his neck to bristle. He had the weirdest idea that someone was watching them. Not that he'd ever tell Marc and Rebecca that, of course.

'Joey's right,' Marc said. 'We have to tell the police about the plane crash.'

'There's something that's worrying me though,' Rebecca said as she started to move out of the Darkfell Ring.

'What's that?' Joey asked and tried to drag his eyes away from the stones.

'That plane, with or without its passengers, crashed – how long ago now?'

Marc shrugged his shoulders. 'Forty minutes or so, I guess,' he said. He still couldn't see where Rebecca was leading and he asked her to explain.

'So where are the emergency services?' she asked. 'You'd've thought that an ambulance would have turned up by now.'

'Looks like I was right after all and no one saw the plane come down,' Marc said.

He turned back to Joey, who was still standing in the centre of the Darkfell Ring, staring silently at the stones.

'You coming, Joey?' Marc asked. Joey didn't reply, and for a moment Marc thought that Joey hadn't heard him.

'Sure, but not to the cops,' he said. 'I sure as anything don't get on with Ashby down at the station. He's one of the guys who wants to stop the rock festival happening, isn't he?'

'Then we'll meet you at Colette's place later,' Marc suggested as Joey raced up to join them.

'OK.' Joey took one final look at the six stones of the Darkfell Ring. 'You know, there is something majorly weird about those muthas. Do you see the way they kind of . . . glow?'

'Glow?'

Rebecca glanced back at the stones. Sure enough, they did seem to be shimmering and sparkling faintly in the afternoon sunlight. 'It's probably just mica deposits catching and reflecting the light from the sun.'

'Either that, or it's fairy dust,' Marc joked.

Laughing, the three of them made their way back down the hill.

But as they did so, they didn't see the shape which detached itself from the long shadow cast by the tall right-hand stone. Joey's feeling had been right. They had indeed been spied upon.

The mysterious watcher was small: a little more than a metre in height. It walked upright like a man, but its long spindly arms almost touched the ground – like those of an ape. And yet there wasn't a patch of hair or fur on its green, naked body. On either side of its large bulbous head there were two small lumps, which might once have been ears.

As Marc, Rebecca and Joey departed, the creature watched them through large, unblinking, reptilian eyes. It chittered softly to itself, showing emotions: excitement; anticipation.

Hunger.

It opened its mouth. Its teeth were razor-sharp. A forked tongue licked its lips.

Greedily.

People like Marc, Rebecca and Joey – their minds young and intelligent, fresh and vibrant – were the creature's favourite food.

For the Time of Returning was almost due and the Demons of the Darkfell Ring were hungry.

And soon once more, just as they had done for so many untold centuries, they would have to feed. But this time, it would be the last and greatest feast of them all.

THE PSYCHIC ZONE

4

Sergeant Ashby on the Case

Dateline: Brentmouth Village Police Station;
Monday 1 June; 15.45.

Police Sergeant Digby Ashby was the sort of man who had much too grand an idea of himself. He was fat and balding, with an age and a waistline in their mid-forties, and he'd never really appreciated working in the tiny village of Brentmouth. He'd much rather have been tracking vicious serial killers down in London instead of helping Miss Stebbins, the postmistress, find her lost cat, or helping Bert Wilkins chuck out the late-night drinkers at *The Witches' Rest*, the local pub.

Because of that, news of the forthcoming rock concert had literally been music to his ears. Not that he'd allow the event to go ahead, of course. He wasn't going to have all those hippies and punks and goths and gypsies and ravers and Brit-poppers and road protesters and screaming teenagers on his patch. But the Zarathustra concert provided him with an opportunity to show people just how important he really was. It might even gain him his long-awaited promotion and a chance to move away from here. Even more important, it could even get him a passing mention on the local TV news.

And when Marc and Rebecca turned up at his tiny police station with news of a crashed plane, he couldn't believe his good luck. Here was yet another chance to show his superiors back at county headquarters just what an efficient and reliable copper he really was.

'I'll have to call over to the town and enlist some of their men,' he informed them. 'Contact the cottage hospital, of course, to take care of the casualties. There's bound to be many.' He licked his lips, almost relishing the prospect of broken and bloody bodies strewn all over the Darkfell Rise.

'But that's just it, Sergeant Ashby,' Rebecca protested. 'There aren't any bodies.'

'Aren't any bodies? Of course, there are bodies, dozens of 'em,' Ashby insisted. 'You just missed them in all the carnage, little lady!'

Don't call me 'little lady'! Rebecca thought.

'There wasn't any "carnage", and it was just a five-seater light aircraft,' Marc corrected him. Ashby wasn't listening. He'd received a severe reprimand from one of his superiors for failing to come up with the culprits behind the recent series of burglaries in the village. Here was a chance to redeem himself. He could already see the newspaper headlines: *Local Bobby Saves Hundreds. Arise, Sir Digby, Saviour of the Shires.* Or even better: *Digby Ashby – The Movie.*

'Now you imagine that this plane was heading for the local airfield?'

It was Rebecca who answered. 'That's right,' she said. 'The staff there will have a list of all the passengers on the plane.'

She shared a look with Marc, and he nodded. It would be pointless telling Ashby about the two brothers on the plane. Ashby wouldn't believe them without seeing the letter, and Joey had taken that with him.

Ashby stood up at his desk, signalling that the meeting was at an end. 'Hurry along, now,' he said as he shooed them out of his office. 'There are emergency services to contact, rescue operations to be put into action.'

'Just one thing, Sergeant,' Marc said as he was ushered through the door. 'Have you decided if the Zarathustra gig is going to be allowed to go ahead yet?'

Ashby scowled. 'That blasted rock and roll concert?' he spluttered. 'Not if I can help it. Scroungers, wasters and troublemakers: every damn one of those blasted pop music fans! Believe me, laddie, that concert will only happen over my own dead body!'

Dateline: Fiveways;
Monday 1 June; 19.25.

'Well, maybe Sergeant Ashby is right after all,' said Colette Russell after Marc, Rebecca and Joey had turned up at her house as planned. Colette was one of their best friends, a pleasant local girl who lived with her parents and a live-in housekeeper at Fiveways, the big old house just on the edge of the village.

Joey groaned. 'Man, oh man, Colette, you're getting to sound just like Rebecca here,' he complained good-naturedly.

'Is that such a problem? I've heard bad things about these rock concerts.'

'Such as?'

'Violence, drugs, crime . . .'

'That's just the picture the tabloids paint,' Marc said confidently, standing up for Joey. 'Festivals are much more organised these days. There's always loads of security just to make sure that things don't get out of hand.'

'Still, even if I did like Zarathustra's music – which I don't–'

'At least you and I have good taste then,' Rebecca cracked.

'You still wouldn't catch me going out on the Darkfell Rise and especially anywhere near the Darkfell Ring,' the younger girl continued. (Rebecca had told her of their earlier visit.) 'I've lived in the area much longer than any of you and I've always hated the place.'

'It's nothing but a collection of old stones,' Rebecca said reasonably. 'What's there to be frightened of?'

'Did you see how the soil is barren inside the Ring? Or the way the stones sometimes seem to glow?' (Here Marc and Joey exchanged a look.) 'It's a spooky place. *Things happen there.*'

'Now you're beginning to sound like Miss Rumford,' Rebecca said. 'She and Marc think the fairies are behind everything.'

'I do not!' Marc insisted once again. Rebecca had been teasing him mercilessly for the better part of the day. He grinned and pretended to take her joke in good part. He certainly wasn't going to give her the satisfaction of winding him up any more.

'There have always been stories of fairies in these parts,' Colette continued. 'And of changelings.'

'Changelings?' asked Joey. 'Now what in the universe are changelings?'

'Another of the old legends,' Marc explained knowledgeably and then blushed red with embarrassment. 'The ... er, the ... um ...'

' "Fairies" is the word you're looking for, big buddy,' Joey said and chuckled to himself.

Marc glowered at him. What chance did he have when both Rebecca and Joey were ganging up on him?

'OK,' he said grumpily. 'The fairies are supposed to come in the night, abduct a human child and replace him or her with one of their own kind.'

'Now I know that you're both mad!' Rebecca said.

'I didn't say I believed in it,' Marc pointed out, quite rightly. 'No matter what you think, I'm not as completely bonkers as old Miss Rumford!'

'Nor did I,' Colette said. 'I was just telling you about the legends, that's all. And besides, Miss Rumford isn't "bonkers", as you put it. People say that she's one of the wisest people in this part of the country. Her family has lived around here for as long as anyone can remember.'

'It's all superstitious twaddle,' Rebecca said. She picked up the newspaper lying on the coffee table in Colette's living room. It was open at the horoscope pages. 'Just like this is. You don't seriously believe in astrology, do you, Colette?'

'Of course not,' Colette said defensively – if not quite truthfully – and shifted awkwardly in her seat. 'It's just a bit of a giggle, that's all.'

'After all, how can anything in the sky influence what happens down here on Earth?'

'The moon affects the tides, Bec,' Marc said. 'And some people say that comets are a sign of evil.'

Rebecca sighed. 'I suppose you're referring to that comet I'm studying up at Fetch Hill?' she asked.

'It was supposedly a comet that wiped out the dinosaurs,' Marc reminded her. 'Maybe your comet's coming to signal the end of all intelligent life here on Earth.'

'Well, at least you'll be safe then,' Rebecca jibed. 'Even you couldn't believe in all that nonsense, Marc!'

'Anyway you can check out Marc's crazy theory up at the radio telescope!' Joey laughed.

'You're going to Fetch Hill tonight?' Colette asked.

'That's right,' Rebecca answered. 'It's part of my

astronomy assignment. Professor Henderson there is letting me use the radio telescope.'

'I don't understand all this scientific stuff,' Colette admitted.

'It's better than believing in spooks and haunted stone circles,' Rebecca said, and added pointedly: 'And astrology columns.'

She looked at her watch. If she didn't make a move now she would be late for her appointment with Professor Henderson, she told them.

'Don't stay out too late,' Colette said. 'Remember you said you'd come with me down to London tomorrow to go shopping.'

'I won't forget,' Rebecca promised her.

'You're sure that's OK?' the younger girl asked anxiously. 'I don't want to interfere with your studies.'

'You won't,' Rebecca reassured her. 'I've the afternoon off, and Mr Boyle is away at some conference tomorrow morning so physics is cancelled. But give us a ring first to check, OK? You never know what I might discover up at Fetch Hill tonight.'

After the older girl had gone, Colette looked at her two friends. 'Rebecca thinks I'm stupid, doesn't she? Reading horoscopes and being afraid of the Darkfell Ring the way I am.'

'Of course she doesn't,' Marc said.

'That Ring's a real weird place,' Joey agreed. 'It sure spooked me out as well.'

'She probably thinks I'm stupid because I don't attend the Institute with all the rest of you.'

'You know she doesn't, Colette,' Marc said.

'Well, I'll show her!' Colette determined. 'I'll prove to Rebecca that I'm just as rational as she is.'

'Hey, chill out, Colette,' Marc told her. 'What are you going to do? Spend a night in a haunted house? Camp out in the Darkfell Ring?'

'Careful the fairies don't get you!' Joey cracked.

'Now you're making fun of me,' Colette pouted. 'Why ever shouldn't I go to the Ring? I'll show you that I'm not scared of anything that might be out there.'

'Rebecca didn't mean anything by it,' Joey told her. 'And anyway we've got more important things to get hassled about at the moment.'

'That's right,' Marc said, eager to change the subject. 'Like what happened to the passengers in that plane.'

'Maybe Ashby and his cops will turn something up by tomorrow morning,' Joey wondered. They'd seen a squad of police cars heading up towards the Darkfell Rise and the crash site just as twilight was falling.

'Yeah, and maybe we'll be able to find out who these Romulus and Remus guys are,' Marc said.

'Perhaps General Axford will know,' Colette suggested. 'You could ask him.'

'Maybe,' Marc said, although he didn't sound too certain.

THE PSYCHIC ZONE

5

Into the Mists

Dateline: Fetch Hill Radio Telescope;
Monday 1 June; 21.25.

Even though it was a good twenty or thirty minutes'
car drive from the village, the Fetch Hill Radio Telescope dominated Brentmouth and the surrounding
countryside. It perched on its hill like a vulture over-
looking its prey.

It wasn't a big affair as these things go. Even the
relatively small telescope up at Jodrell Bank was much
larger. But it was certainly powerful, receiving radio
emissions from objects many thousands of light years
away from the Earth.

Rebecca always felt a special thrill when she got
off the bus at the foot of the hill. She felt dwarfed,
and not just by Fetch Hill itself (even Rebecca had
heard the local legends which said that witches

had once celebrated their sabbats on the hill).

The telescope's giant dish, with its antenna pointing out to space, seemed to be on the very cutting edge of science. It was reaching out to an unknown universe, much farther than any human had ever done before. Who knew what it might find out there?

Nestled around the base of the telescope, like ducklings around their mother, stood a series of small concrete buildings. These were the control buildings, in which scientists laboured, evaluating all the data received by the telescope, and trying to make sense of it.

Rebecca was working there now with Professor Henderson, a tall, reedy man in his late forties. They were studying a series of data which had just come in this morning. All around them, other white-coated technicians were working late, studying the messages coming in from the night sky.

Rebecca had placed the read-outs of radio emissions alongside photographs taken by Fetch Hill's other telescope, a more conventional optical telescope. Against the backdrop of stars there was a thin streak of light: the new comet which was heading towards Earth.

She jabbed a finger at a series of figures. According to this new information, the comet had started to emit a strange new series of regular and very powerful radio pulses – altogether different from the pulses it had been giving out when it had first been detected. And that, of course, was impossible.

'Everyone's noticed it,' Henderson said. 'Jodrell Bank, Arecibo, the whole lot.'

'Could it be some sort of freak effect?' Rebecca suggested. 'Maybe interference from a quasar or even a black hole?'

'Not at this power,' Henderson said and traced with a long, grubby finger the wavy line on the computer-generated graph, outlining the highs and the lows of the radio emissions. 'These are definitely coming from the comet. And see how regular these pulses are. That's unusual.'

Rebecca frowned. 'You're not saying that they're artificial?' she asked.

Henderson smiled. 'I didn't say that,' he said. 'As far as we're concerned it's still just a comet, if one that's a little unusual. We'll know more when it's closer to Earth in a couple of weeks' time.'

Rebecca studied the black-and-white print-out of the night sky which had been taken through the optical telescope. Henderson pointed out for her a certain area.

'It seems to be coming from that part of the sky, near to the star we call Antares,' he told her.

Rebecca examined the print more closely. 'Somewhere in the constellation of Scorpio then,' she said and then smiled to herself. 'Thank goodness Colette isn't here. She'd probably read some deep astrological significance into that!'

Henderson started to shrug off his white lab coat, and he gathered up his papers. He was going to have an early night, he told Rebecca.

'Aren't you interested in the new comet?' she asked, surprised.

'Of course, but there are more important things than the comet at the moment,' he told her with a twinkle in his eye.

'There are?'

'Of course,' Henderson smiled. 'My collection of Zarathustra on vinyl! Rebecca, I can't wait for the concert.'

'Not you as well!' Rebecca despaired. 'Am I the only sane person on this planet?'

'Very probably,' Henderson laughed. 'The astronomers who first detected the comet have even changed its name.'

'Thank goodness for that then,' Rebecca said. New comets were usually named after the scientists who first discovered them. In this case, it had been called after two Polish astronomers with particularly unpronounceable names.

'It seems that they're music fans as well,' Henderson said, as he made his way out of the room. 'They've renamed it Comet Zarathustra, in honour of the concert!'

'Now I know that the world is going mad,' Rebecca sighed and returned to her work.

Dateline: The Darkfell Ring;
Monday 1 June; 23.58.

The summer wind blew Colette's blonde hair into her eyes as she approached the Darkfell Ring. It had taken all her courage to come even this far, catching a cab to the foot of the Darkfell Rise, and then walking the final stretch of hill by herself.

But she had to prove something, not just to Rebecca and to the others, but to herself as well. She had to prove that she wasn't scared. Rebecca had laughed at her. Now she had to prove that she didn't believe all that superstitious nonsense Rebecca had accused her of.

The moon was full in the night sky. The six stones of the Darkfell Ring stood silhouetted against its white O-shape. One of the old legends said that the six stones of the Ring were the bodies of evil-doers who had been magically transformed into stone. Now, with the wind whistling spookily through the Ring, Colette could quite easily believe that.

She entered the Darkfell Ring. Was it her imagination, or were the stones glowing, twinkling with an eerie and mysterious light? Of course it was her imagination! After all, they were just lumps of rock.

Weren't they?

Long ago, people had worshipped here, within this enchanted circle. Even today, there were those who still celebrated the summer and the winter solstices. Colette could feel the presence of all those people down through the years. It was as if the stones had somehow soaked up their presence. It was as if they had absorbed their very souls, like ink soaked up by blotting paper. She looked once more at the stones. Could she see faces in them? Or was that just a weird effect of the moonlight and the shadows?

Of course it was.

Wasn't it?

From far off she thought she could hear a rumbling sound. Approaching thunder.

Wasn't it?

As she listened, the noise seemed to come closer – seemed to shake the very ground on which she was standing. That very ground which had not borne flowers or plants since before anyone could remember.

Colette took a few deep breaths and tried to control her nerves. She had to face her fear, she kept on telling herself that. She had to prove that there was nothing to be scared of. She had to prove that there were no such things as ghosts. She had to prove that–

Her breath caught in her throat. She looked at the stones more closely. She had been right! It had not been her imagination! They *were* glowing! With an evil, unearthly light! And the two stones that were glowing the strongest, almost blinding her with their brilliance, were the altar stone and the Needle's Eye.

It was her imagination. She kept on repeating that to herself, over and over again in her head.

No. No. No. This is real. That was what her heart told her.

Down in Brentmouth village the clock tower of Saint Michael's church tolled twelve. Midnight: the witching hour.

A strange mist sprang up from out of nowhere. A thick, green fog, curling around the stones of the Darkfell Ring. An evil, unearthly fog.

Unearthly.

It made it difficult to see. It stung Colette's eyes. They began to water. Her vision became blurred. She started to feel woozy. The world began to spin sickeningly around her.

Colette was suddenly aware of another presence nearby. She looked in the direction of the largest stone. There was a light emanating from the headstone, and someone – no, some*thing* – was coming towards her.

She couldn't make out its features, only its general shape. A thin, emaciated body. Long spindly arms and legs. It didn't quite walk upright but shuffled along in a hunched position, like an old, old man.

Then there was another brief flash of light from one of the other stones. She saw the creature's large head – much too big for the rest of its body. A small mouth. A long forked tongue. No eyelids, no eyebrows. No features to make it recognisably human. Two staring, unblinking eyes: watching her.

Colette wanted to run. Her legs refused to move. Could the mists have somehow paralysed her and frozen her to the spot? Who cared? Colette knew that she was a prisoner, captured by the alien powers of the Darkfell Ring.

Colette watched on in horror. The creature reached out for her with six long and bony fingers. When they touched her arm, she felt them burn through the thick cloth of her jacket.

The creature pulled her towards it. Colette couldn't resist. The mists were thicker now and she breathed them in. She thought she would choke. She remembered the time when she was small and she had been learning to swim. Then she was sure that she was going to drown. That was how it felt now.

The next thing she knew, she was lying down on some sort of operating table. The green mist still hung all around her.

Creatures similar to her captor stood around the table, examining her like she was an animal in a zoo. They were stroking their pointed chins thoughtfully. Chattering amongst themselves in a language she didn't recognise – if it was a proper language at all. The sounds they made reminded her much more of the chirruping of crickets or of grasshoppers.

An alien hand touched her cheek and Colette tried to turn away in revulsion. She couldn't move at all. The mists had frozen her limbs.

She wanted to run away – she couldn't.

She tried to scream – no sound came from her lips.

And then Colette did the most sensible thing she could have done. She fainted dead away and slipped into welcome unconsciousness.

THE PSYCHIC ZONE

6

New Arrivals

*Dateline: The Institute, Biology Lab 2B;
Tuesday 2 June; 11.15.*

'Marc, I can't contact Colette.'

Rebecca had managed to track Marc down to one of the biology labs. He was sitting at a workbench and peering down into a large glass case lit by an overhead lamp.

Marc looked up, seemingly unconcerned. 'Is that a problem?' he asked.

'Remember we were supposed to be going down to London this morning?' she reminded him.

'How could I forget?' Marc sighed. 'What is it with you girls? You get a day off and you decide to spend it shopping. Can't you think of anything more productive – like having a lie-in?'

Rebecca ignored the jibe. 'I rang her house this

morning, and the housekeeper, Miss Kerr, told me that no one was at home.'

'Aren't her folks there?' Marc asked.

'No. They're off on some sort of business trip.'

For a moment Marc was worried. Then he smiled. 'Colette can look after herself,' he reassured her. 'She probably thought that you'd want to spend more time at Fetch Hill, and so she went off on her own.'

'But why didn't she tell the housekeeper?' Rebecca asked.

'She must have forgotten, that's all,' Marc said. 'I thought I was supposed to be the suspicious one amongst us. But if it makes you any happier we can call on her at lunchtime. Joey and I want to go and see what's happening about that plane up on Darkfell Rise: see how many thousands of bodies Ashby has pulled out of the wreckage single-handedly!'

Rebecca lightened up a little. Marc could always make her seen the funny side of things. She peered into the glass case. Inside, on an old piece of tree bark, two lizards were basking in the heat from the over-head lamp.

'Yuk,' was her decidedly unscientific comment. 'What are those two ugly-looking things?'

Marc seemed hurt, and he prodded one of the lizards with a stick. The creature looked balefully at him, clearly irritated at being disturbed.

'Chameleons. And I think they're beautiful.'

'You're weird.'

'They're brilliant masters of disguise,' he told her

enthusiastically. 'They change their colour to fit in with their environment.'

'Whatever for?' Rebecca asked.

'To protect themselves from predators,' he told her.

'Well, I still think they're ugly.' She changed the subject. 'Have you talked to General Axford about the letter we found?'

'Not yet,' Marc said. 'I've got an appointment with him in ten minutes' time. You want to come along?'

Rebecca said that she did. 'But won't Eva be there?' she asked. Marc shook his head.

'No, I checked,' he told her. 'She's off to the train station to pick up a couple of new pupils who are starting next term.'

Rebecca whistled appreciatively. 'Wow. An audience with the General without his personal assistant breathing down his neck. That is something! He's always much nicer and more forthcoming when she isn't around.'

Marc checked his watch and stood up. 'Let's go and see him then,' he said. He took one final look at the chameleons in the glass case. ''Bye, my pretties,' he said jokingly. 'I wish I could disguise myself as well as you two when my biology homework's overdue!'

Dateline: The Institute, General Axford's Office;
Tuesday 2 June; 12.00.

General Axford, the principal of the Institute, was a gaunt man with a sallow complexion, hollow cheeks and thin, greying hair. But it was his startlingly blue eyes which always made Rebecca and Marc feel uneasy. They never revealed what he was really thinking, yet at the same time they seemed to be able to probe deep into their own minds. Even though he was now in a wheelchair (the result of a mysterious accident which had confined him to a private hospital several months ago) he was still an imposing presence.

'So, you say that two boys were in this plane that crashed over on the Rise?' he asked. 'Now that is hardly likely, is it? If so, where are their bodies? People don't just vanish in mid-air, now, do they?'

Marc and Rebecca shuffled awkwardly in their chairs in front of Axford's desk. The General had a habit of making everyone who met him feel very foolish indeed.

'There was a letter in the wreckage confirming that they had enrolled here at the Institute,' Marc said.

Axford arched an eyebrow in interest. 'And of course you have this letter on you, Mr Price?'

Marc cursed himself. He'd forgotten to take the letter from Joey last night as he had planned.

'So you present me with no evidence, only a fanciful notion that two boys, who might just have enrolled at the Institute, might just have been flying in that plane?'

Axford said superiorly. 'I expect such flights of fancy from you, Mr Price, but certainly not you, Miss Storm.'

Rebecca sprang loyally to Marc's defence. 'We can produce the letter, General,' she assured him. 'But in the meantime can you recall anyone with those boys' names being enrolled recently?'

Axford shook his head. 'Eva now deals with all new admissions to the Institute,' he reminded them. He frowned; it was obviously something of a sore point with him. 'She took over the responsibility when I was hospitalised following my unfortunate accident,' he said, and looked down at his two paralysed legs. 'Even now she's collecting two new students from the railway station.'

'Sir, what could have happened to the passengers in the plane?' Rebecca asked General Axford one last time.

'I would have thought it apparent, Miss Storm,' Axford said. There was now a slight edge to his voice and it was obvious that he thought Rebecca and Marc were wasting his time. 'They survived the crash and simply walked away.'

'No sir,' Marc said, and Axford glared angrily at him. 'They couldn't have escaped alive from that wreckage.'

'You said that the plane was a military aircraft,' Axford reminded them. 'Has it never occurred to you that the pilot may just have parachuted out when he discovered that he was losing control?'

'That's not particularly likely, is it?' Marc said, earning yet another angry look from Axford. 'And even if he did, what about these two boys? I can't imagine a couple of schoolkids baling out without sustaining some kind of injury.'

'You have no evidence that there were any school-children in the plane at all,' Axford said sternly.

'But the letter –' Rebecca began, before Axford interrupted her.

'A letter which I have not yet seen,' he said. 'And even if it does exist, that doesn't prove that – what were the names of these two boys again?'

'Romulus and Remus Hawthorne,' Rebecca reminded him.

'It doesn't prove that they were actually on board,' Axford concluded. 'Now, might I suggest that you return to your studies at the Institute?'

'But –'

'That is enough, Mr Price!' Axford declared angrily. He was about to say something else, when there was a knock at the door of his office. 'Enter!'

The door opened and Eva marched in. As usual, the tall, short-haired blonde was wearing her stark black power suit, and the dark glasses which hid her eyes even on the most overcast days. She looked scornfully at Marc and Rebecca before turning to Axford.

'I'm sorry, General, I wasn't aware that you were in a meeting,' she said. Marc and Rebecca weren't fooled for an instant. In their experience, there was very little Eva wasn't aware of.

'That's quite all right, Eva. Miss Storm and Mr Price were just leaving, weren't you?'

Marc and Rebecca took the point and stood up to

go. As they did so, they noticed for the first time the two people standing behind Eva.

'I thought you might like to meet the new arrivals, General,' Eva said and called the newcomers forward.

The two boys seemed to be in their mid-teens and were identical in every respect. They each had blond hair (as blond as Eva's, Marc thought), which flopped over their large eyes, a peaches-and-cream complexion, and pleasant, open faces. They were also dressed in smartly tailored jackets and trousers – a rare sight at the Institute, where most of the students slopped around in baggy sweatshirts and jeans. They looked just like your typical English public-schoolboys, Rebecca thought.

'Might I present the twins Romulus and Remus Hawthorne to you, General Axford?' Eva said. She smiled her usual cold smile. 'They are our latest recruits to the Institute. I've just collected them from the train station.'

Romulus and Remus strode forwards to shake the General's hand and then reached out to greet Rebecca and Marc.

Marc winced as Romulus – or Remus, he wasn't quite sure which – took his hand. The boy looked slight, but his grip was so firm that it almost hurt. His hand felt cold and clammy to the touch. His eyes were unnaturally large. The pupils weren't quite round, but almost slit-like, and they reminded him of something . . . something he couldn't quite put his finger on.

'I am so pleased to meet you, Marc,' the boy said. His manner was strangely formal and he spoke with a slight lisp. 'I hope that we can be friends as well as colleagues here at the Institute.'

'Yeah, sure,' Marc said.

Behind his desk General Axford chuckled superiorly. 'So much for your fairy stories, Mr Price,' he said.

As soon as they had left Axford's office, Rebecca turned to Marc. 'Well, we've just gone and made complete idiots of ourselves, haven't we?' she said. 'It looks like the General was right and those guys weren't on the plane after all.'

'Maybe,' said Marc who wasn't quite sure. 'But it still doesn't explain what happened to the pilot. We all saw how that plane went out of control. I don't believe he'd've had time to bale out.'

'Then we'll just have to find out what really happened,' Rebecca said.

'Thanks for the "we",' Marc said and then shuddered. 'What did you think of those two guys? I never thought I'd say it, but they gave me the creeps even more than Eva does!'

'There was something strange about them, yes,' Rebecca agreed. 'Especially their eyes. Did you see the way they were always flicking back and forth, and were never still? And those funny-shaped pupils of theirs?'

Marc nodded. 'I've just remembered where I've seen eyes like that before,' he said darkly.

'Where?'

'Back in the biology lab,' he reminded her. 'We both saw them. They've got eyes just like my chameleons – just like lizards . . .'

THE PSYCHIC ZONE

7

A Man Called Smith

Dateline: The Darkfell Rise;
Tuesday 2 June; 14.45.

After their meeting with Axford, Marc and Rebecca picked Joey up at the on-site boys' hostel where he lived, and they all made their way up to Darkfell Rise and the site of the plane crash. Marc promised that afterwards they'd check up on Colette.

'You know I could always zap her and find out where she is!' Joey said, as they climbed the hill. In the distance they could see a group of men milling around the Rise.

'Zap her?' Rebecca said and made a face. 'Am I going to regret asking you what you're talking about, Joey?'

Joey tapped the side of his head. 'Like make telepathic contact with her?' he suggested.

'I thought we'd agreed not to talk too freely about those powers,' Marc said warily. He looked around to see if anyone else was listening, and then realised how foolish he was being. Who could be eavesdropping on them up here on the Darkfell Rise?

'I don't see why not,' Joey said, and sulked a little. He'd lately been feeling much more comfortable with his telepathic abilities, and sometimes couldn't quite understand why Marc and Rebecca had insisted that they remain their secret.

'Can you imagine what would happen if the General or Eva found out about them?' Rebecca asked.

'Remember the Project, Joey,' Marc reminded him.

'OK, point taken,' Joey said, and winced at the memory of the mysterious organisation which had kidnapped him on his arrival in England. They had somehow discovered his psychic abilities and had intended to force him to use them to wreak havoc and destruction throughout the world.

'You couldn't zap me anyway,' Rebecca said.

'Sure, I know that I can't zap you two,' Joey said airily.

'We must be thankful for small mercies then,' Rebecca said sarcastically. She didn't fancy having Joey read her own thoughts.

'But Colette, well, she's more sensitive than you two are,' he continued. 'I can always get a feeling of where she is, if I try hard enough.'

Marc grinned. 'I think we'll use slightly more conventional measures, Joey!' he said. He stopped and frowned, and then drew the others' attention to what

was happening ahead of them up on the side of
Darkfell Rise.

About twenty men in black suits were milling about
the area where the plane had crashed. Some were
carrying clipboards and taking notes. Others were
scanning the area with what Rebecca recognised were
portable Geiger counters. A further group were bark-
ing orders into mobile phones and two-way radios.

'It looks like Sergeant Ashby got his act together
after all,' Marc said.

'They're not the cops,' Joey realised.

'And how do you know?' Rebecca asked. 'They
could be in plain clothes.'

Joey shook his head. 'When you've hung around
Harlem as much as I've done you can spot a cop a
mile off, plain-clothes or not!'

'Then we'll bow to your superior wisdom,' Rebecca
said wryly. She, too, had been born in New York City,
but in a neighbourhood a million times more upmarket
than Joey's. 'So if they're not cops who are they?'

'Hang on, you two,' Marc said. 'Haven't you
noticed something important here?'

'Such as?' asked Rebecca.

'Where's the plane?'

Marc was right. The wreckage from yesterday had
been cleared away. Apart from a small patch of
scorched grass and the broken branches of some trees
a little way off, there was no sign that anything had
ever crashed down here.

'Let's go and ask,' Rebecca suggested, but Joey was
more cautious.

'Guys, I'm not sure that I like this,' he said. Before he could say anything more they were spotted by one of the men in black suits. He came over to them.

'What are you kids doing here?' he demanded. The man was tall and slim, and handsome in a slightly severe way. Marc judged him to be in his mid to late-thirties. He was smartly dressed and had slicked-back black hair. He was wearing a pair of sunglasses.

'What's happened to the plane?' Marc demanded. Beside him, Rebecca sighed. Subtlety had never been Marc's strong point, and he always tended to ask questions without thinking of the possible conse-quences.

The man looked curiously at the three of them. 'What do you know about a crashed plane?' he demanded.

'We could hardly fail to miss it,' Joey said.

'Are you the kids who told Ashby about the crash?'

'No,' Rebecca replied quickly before either of the others had the opportunity to answer. 'But news travels fast in a village as small as this one. Were many people hurt?'

The man considered Rebecca carefully. She wasn't sure whether he believed her or not. Finally he answered, 'All the passengers were killed.'

'Oh no, that's terrible!' she said. She hoped she sounded convincing enough.

'The pilot and his two passengers,' the man lied. 'Their bodies have been shipped off to the local morgue. The wreckage has been taken for analysis.'

'Where to?' Joey asked.

'Just why are you so interested?' The man was suspicious now.

'He's just being nosey, that's all,' Marc answered on Joey's behalf.

'Keep out of things which don't concern you.'

Is that a threat, buster? Joey thought. What he said, however, was, 'Sorry,' and then he hung his head guiltily.

'We don't like people who ask too many questions, OK?'

Yup, thought Joey, *that most definitely was a threat!*

The man whipped an ID card out of his jacket pocket and flashed it in front of their faces. Marc read the words printed on it: *General John Smith. Ministry of Defence*.

Rebecca smiled sweetly at Smith. 'We're sorry if we've interrupted you,' she said in her best little-girl voice, and fluttered her eyelashes at him. 'We didn't mean any harm.'

Smith smiled back. His smile didn't make him look any less sinister. 'Then there's no harm done, is there?' he said. 'But keep away from here, OK? There's nothing for you here.'

'Of course we will,' Rebecca promised him and led Marc and Joey back down the hill.

'Rebecca Storm, that was the most shameless display of feminine wiles I've ever seen in my life! You should be totally disgusted with yourself!' Marc said, full of admiration.

'It got him off our backs, didn't it?' Rebecca said. 'Who do you think he was?'

'John Smith!' Joey sneered. 'At least he could have been a little more original than that!'

'Do you suppose he really was with the MoD?' Rebecca asked.

Marc shrugged. 'Maybe. Maybe not,' he replied. 'But one thing's for certain. He was lying. We know for a fact that there weren't any bodies in that wreckage. And he didn't want anyone to investigate the scene of the crash.'

'Why would the Government want to cover up something like this?' Rebecca wondered.

'If he *was* with the Government,' Marc continued. 'Maybe he's had the wreckage removed so the Government won't find out what really happened to that plane and its passengers.'

Dateline: Fiveways;
Tuesday 2 June; 17.05.

The live-in housekeeper at Fiveways, the big house on the edge of the village, was close to tears. With Colette's father and mother away so often, she was responsible for looking after Colette. Now she felt that she was the reason behind the girl's disappearance, and she told Rebecca, Marc and Joey so.

'Hey, relax, Miss Kerr,' Marc said. He put a reassuring arm around the woman's shoulder. 'She's probably just gone down to London like she said she would.'

Miss Kerr wasn't so sure. 'Then why didn't she tell me?' she needed to know.

'Miss Kerr, do you think I could go up to Colette's bedroom for a minute?' Rebecca asked.

'Of course. But whatever for?'

'Er, I lent Colette one of my CDs last week,' Rebecca lied. 'She said she'd return it but she kept on forgetting.'

'Maybe she left it downstairs in the kitchen,' Miss Kerr said helpfully, glad for anything to take her mind off Colette's disappearance. 'What was it called?'

Rebecca thought fast. '*The Best of Zarathustra*,' she said. Marc and Joey exchanged puzzled looks. 'Have you seen it, Miss Kerr?'

Miss Kerr thought hard. 'No,' she said finally. She told Rebecca that she was free to look in Colette's room if she wanted.

Rebecca went upstairs and returned a few minutes later. She shrugged her shoulders. 'I couldn't find it,' she told the housekeeper and the two boys. 'It looks like I'll have to wait until she gets back.'

'If she ever does,' Miss Kerr said gloomily.

'Chill out, Miss Kerr!' Marc said cheerfully. 'She'll be back before you know it! She's probably round at Bec's, dropping off the CD right now, and chatting to Bec's mum!'

'Of course she is!' Rebecca said. Unlike Marc and Joey and most Institute students, Rebecca still lived at home with her mother, who had moved to the area especially so that her daughter could attend the exclusive school. 'She knows that Zarathustra are my favourite band at the moment. I can't wait for their concert up there on the Darkfell Rise!'

Rebecca made her goodbyes and left the house with Marc and Joey. As soon as they had closed the door, Marc turned on Rebecca.

'OK, Bec, come clean! What are you up to?' he asked her. 'First of all, Zarathustra is the last band in the world Colette would be interested in!'

'Yeah, she always did have abysmal taste,' Joey added. 'Who is that Mozart guy she keeps listening to anyway?'

Marc ignored the comment. 'And secondly, you saying that Zarathustra's your favourite band is a bit like Madonna saying she's going to enter a convent,' he carried on. ' "A bunch of forty-somethings making clowns out of themselves", I seem to remember you calling them only yesterday!'

'Relax, guys,' she told them. 'I only said that so I could get Miss Kerr to let me snoop into Colette's room.'

'And what did you find out?' Joey asked.

'Only that her bed hasn't been slept in all night,' Rebecca replied.

Marc's face fell and he turned to Joey. 'You don't think she went to the Darkfell Ring like she said she would?' he asked him.

'What are you two talking about?' Rebecca wanted to know. Joey told her about their good-natured teasing of Colette and her determination that she'd show them that she was no coward.

'You idiots! Anything could happen to her up

on Darkfell Rise at that time of night!'

'Hey, Bec, we didn't mean any harm,' Marc said, even though he knew that Rebecca was right and that both he and Joey had acted like fools. 'We were only having a bit of fun with her, that was all!'

'Well, that settles it. We go to the police and report her missing.'

'Isn't that being a little bit hasty?' Joey said.

'No, it's not.'

'There could be a thousand and one reasons why she didn't sleep in her bed last night.'

'Such as?'

Marc shrugged his shoulders. 'Perhaps she stayed with a friend down in the village last night?' he suggested.

'Without telling Miss Kerr?' Rebecca said. 'Do you really believe that?'

'OK, maybe not.'

'Right, we go to the police.'

Dateline: Brentmouth Police Station;
Tuesday 2 June; 18.10.

When the three of them reached the police station, they found Sergeant Ashby in his office, packing up all his personal belongings into a cardboard box.

'What's going on?' Marc asked.

'I'm leaving, that's what's going on,' Ashby replied in a voice which could scarcely conceal his delight. 'Leaving Brentmouth for good!'

'I don't understand,' said Rebecca.

'It's very simple,' Ashby said as he placed a signed photograph of Margaret Thatcher into the box. 'I've been given an immediate transfer.'

'A transfer?' asked Joey. 'Where to? Why?'

'The big city,' Ashby said proudly. 'Seems that my superiors have finally recognised my talents. And not before time, I might add.'

Marc and Rebecca looked bemused. They'd imagined Sergeant Ashby staying in the village until his retirement. He certainly wasn't the sort of policeman cut out for life in the Met.

'Pleased with my handling of that plane crash, they were,' he told them.

'And all those hundreds of people you saved from the blazing wreckage?' Marc said wickedly, unable to resist the jibe.

Ashby coloured slightly. 'Well, maybe I exaggerated a little there,' he admitted sheepishly. 'Apparently there were only three bodies in the wreckage. Dead, every one of them. Sad business.'

'Apparently?' Rebecca asked. 'You didn't see the bodies then?'

This was obviously a sore point with Ashby. 'Unfortunately not,' he said, with evident disappointment. 'The Ministry dealt with the crash.'

'Why?' Rebecca asked.

'It was a military plane, of course.'

'Of course,' said Rebecca.

'General Smith was most impressed with me,'

Ashby said, his chest swelling with pride. 'Wasted no time in recommending me for promotion with his friends in the Home Office. I must say I was surprised how quickly he got things moving. But then that's the big city way for you, isn't it? They never let the grass grow beneath their feet.'

'Sure,' said Marc and frowned. From what he knew, the wheels of Government moved with all the speed of a comatose tortoise. What sort of power or influence did this John Smith – if that really was his name – possess?

'And I'm sure that you'll be more than pleased to see me go,' Ashby continued.

'Of course we won't.'

'Of course you will, little lady,' Ashby insisted, not fooled for a moment. 'After all, now that I'm leaving the village, your precious hippy rock festival will go ahead.'

'Zarathustra will be playing after all!' Joey exclaimed and clapped his hands together in excitement. 'Man, now is that ever the best news I've heard in a long time!'

'The man who's been appointed to take over from me – Sadler, a much younger fellow, and not quite up to it, if you want my opinion –'

'We don't,' Marc said impolitely.

'My successor has agreed to give permission for the concert to go ahead,' Ashby continued. He looked intently at the three of them. 'Now, what is it you want with me? I haven't time to waste, you know.'

'It's our friend, Colette Russell,' Rebecca began. 'We think she's gone missing.'

'We haven't seen her since last night,' Joey added.

Ashby yawned. This wasn't something which part-icularly interested him. 'Young girls go missing all the time,' he said nonchalantly. 'I'm sure she'll turn up.'

'Hey, Colette isn't just any young girl,' Joey pro-tested.

'This isn't something she does normally,' Rebecca added.

'Can't do anything until she's been gone for twenty-four hours,' Ashby said.

'But you'll have left by then!' Marc said.

'So take it up with my replacement,' Ashby sug-gested. 'He'll be assuming his post the day after tomorrow.'

'But –' Marc started to protest, when the door to Ashby's office was opened and a young WPC popped her head round the door. There was someone to see him, she said, and the newcomer followed her into the office.

'Colette!' Rebecca rushed forward to hug her. 'We thought you'd gone missing.'

'Hey, now is that trendy or what?' Joey said when he saw the stylish dark glasses that Colette was wearing.

Colette touched the frame of her glasses in a slightly self-conscious gesture. 'I've just been to my optomet-rist,' she told them all. 'He says I've got to wear these for a few weeks. I've got some infection in my eyes.'

'Optometrist?' Marc asked. 'What about your shop-ping trip?'

'Shopping trip?'

'Yes, we thought you'd gone on your own down to

London,' Rebecca reminded her. 'That's where we said we were going today.'

Colette hesitated a half-second before answering. 'Did I? I forgot about the optometrist appointment.'

'Of course,' said Joey.

He looked curiously at Colette. Joey noticed more things than most other people and there was something different about Colette. He couldn't quite put his finger on it, but it was certainly not just those new dark glasses.

'I got home and Miss Kerr told me that you'd all come here,' Colette said. 'Whyever are you all fussing over me?'

Rebecca smiled weakly. 'It's OK, Colette, I think we've just made fools of ourselves again, that's all.'

'I could have you all arrested for wasting police time, you know,' Ashby pointed out.

'Come on, Sergeant,' Marc said cheerily. 'Do you want your last job at Brentmouth to be charging three irritating little kids like us?'

'Yes, just think of the paperwork involved,' Rebecca said. 'Charge sheets in triplicate, contacting our parents!'

'Dealing with Eva at the Institute,' Marc put in.

'Why, there might even be so much of it to do that you'd still be in Brentmouth when Zarathustra perform!' Joey chuckled.

'And we all know how much you like them,' Marc finished for them all.

Ashby saw the good sense of Marc's argument, and dismissed them. As they left the police station, Colette turned to them all with an excited look on her face.

'Zarathustra are playing after all?' she asked.

'That's right – more's the pity,' Rebecca said glumly. She told Colette how Ashby's successor was going to allow the concert to go ahead.

'That's wonderful,' she said. Marc looked strangely at her.

'I guess we've got to thank General Smith – whoever he is,' Marc continued. 'If he hadn't promoted Ashby, the gig wouldn't be happening. He's indirectly responsible for the whole thing happening.'

'Marc,' said Colette. 'I can't wait!'

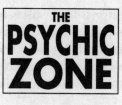

THE PSYCHIC ZONE

8

The Comet Approaches

Dateline: The Institute;
Wednesday 24 June; 15.37.

Life went on as usual at the Institute, but now there was a new hot topic of conversation to take everyone's minds off homework assignments and the diabolically inedible state of school lunches.

The forthcoming concert by Zarathustra had split the school into two opposing camps. There were those who were great fans of the legendary rock band and were counting the days until the outfit made their long-awaited comeback performance in the shadows of the Darkfell Ring.

Then there were the others, who considered that the prospect of a performance by a bunch of jaded has-beens was about as exciting as Old Mother Smythe's physics demonstrations.

Rebecca, not surprisingly, still belonged fairly and squarely to the second group. She told Marc as much when they had finished classes for the day. They were making their way down the corridor to the exit, past posters pinned to the school noticeboard advertising the gig.

'If I hear one more word from anyone about this crummy concert then I swear I am going to scream!' she said. Marc had just given her a tuneless rendition of the band's last hit from over twenty years ago.

Marc wagged a disapproving finger in her face. 'Now, now, now, Bec,' he teased. 'That's hardly the reaction of a sensible and level-headed scientist, is it?'

'Neither is punching you in the ribs, but I will do if you don't stop carrying on about them,' she said. 'Ever since that new police sergeant, Sadler, gave the go-ahead for the gig it seems to be the sole topic of conversation here and in the village.'

'Well, Zarathustra are big news,' Marc said. 'Feelings are bound to run high. Even old Axford's showing a bit of emotion for once in his life!'

'Don't I know it,' Rebecca smiled. 'He's dead-set against the gig, isn't he? Just like your dotty old Miss Rumford.'

'Miss Rumford isn't so dotty,' Marc said. 'Have you seen the poster campaign she's started in the village? *Popsters Go Home*, they all say.'

'Popsters?' Rebecca said, and grimaced.

'Give her a break,' Marc grinned. 'She's only trying to be trendy.'

'Sure she is – trendy for the eighties, that is,'

Rebecca chuckled. 'Even Prof Henderson up at Fetch Hill is getting in on the act. He goes home every night and listens to all his old vinyls of the band.'

'You still working up at the radio telescope?' Marc asked. 'I thought your astronomy assignment was due to be handed in a couple of weeks ago.'

'It was, and I did,' Rebecca told him, and then added casually: 'I got an A-plus.'

'You would,' Marc said grumpily. His grades had been falling lately. For him a simple 'B' would have been cause for a major celebration.

'But I'm still examining that new comet. They've named it Zarathustra, can you believe it?' Rebecca continued. 'I told Henderson I'd like to check it out further.'

'What's so special about it?' Marc asked, as they paused by a poster advertising the forthcoming gig. *Zarathustra – the Reunion*, it read. *Free entry for all accredited students of the Brentmouth Institute for Gifted Youngsters*.

'Nothing much,' Rebecca replied. 'But if my latest calculations are correct –'

'Which they always are,' Marc put in, a little jealously.

Rebecca hid a smug smile. '*If* my calculations are correct then this is the nearest the comet's come to Earth for about six or seven thousand years.'

'So the last time the comet was around was about the time the Darkfell Ring was being built,' he said, and then added brightly: 'Hey, are you thinking what I'm thinking?'

'Sure,' Rebecca said sarcastically and added: 'and there are fairies at the bottom of my garden as well.'

'OK, OK, point taken,' Marc said. He'd no wish to be reminded of his conversation of a few weeks ago with Miss Rumford. He looked up at the poster. 'This is going to be one of the biggest rock events of the past twenty years. The promoters stand to make millions out of it. I wonder why they're giving free entry to students at the Institute?'

'I don't know and I don't care,' Rebecca said. She checked her watch. 'I'll be doing much more important things when that bunch of no-hopers are playing.'

'Watching your comet, I guess?' Marc said. 'As Henderson's at home reliving his youth, I suppose you've got free access to the radio telescope?'

'Something like that,' she confirmed. 'Although one of his assistants is always on hand just to make sure that I don't screw up any of his valuable equipment.'

'I can't imagine you ever doing that. You're far too precise, methodical and grown-up.'

'Thank you.'

'It wasn't exactly meant as a compliment,' Marc corrected her with a smile and then gave her a friendly slap on the shoulder to show that he was joking.

Rebecca was about to say something to Marc when they turned a corner. A small boy was being picked on by two older boys. The younger boy they both recognised as Peter Lee, a pleasant if slightly shy and uncertain thirteen-year-old student. The older boys who were bullying him were the twins, Romulus and Remus.

'Hey, you two, cut that out!' Marc cried. He walked forward to Peter's defence.

'Yes, pick on someone your own age!' Rebecca said, and joined Marc.

The twins released Peter and turned towards Marc and Rebecca. They smiled a superior smile and looked contemptuously at the newcomers.

'And if we refuse?' Romulus asked.

'Yes, what then?' Remus said, and sneered.

Marc saw red and clenched his fists. He took a step towards the nearer of the two twins. He would probably have hit him if Rebecca hadn't laid a restraining hand on his shoulder.

'Marc, leave it.'

'Yes, leave it,' agreed Remus.

'If you know what's good for you,' added Romulus.

Marc glanced at Peter and told him to leave. Peter needed no further encouragement and ran off down the corridor. The twins made no attempt to follow him, but just laughed as they watched him disappear around the corner.

'Just what gives you the right to go around treating people like that?' Marc said. He took a few deep breaths to calm himself down. He hated bullying of all sorts.

'We've got every right,' Romulus said.

'And there's nothing that you can do about it,' Remus added.

In fact, there certainly was something Marc could have done about it. At the moment, there was nothing in the world he would have liked to have done more than punch each of the twins in the face. Yet he knew that doing that would just have brought him down to their own level, and he wasn't prepared to give them that satisfaction.

'I can report you to General Axford,' he said. He became even more irritated when the twins just laughed at him.

'You're hardly Axford's favourite student,' Romulus said.

'Or Eva's,' said Remus.

'The General expects high standards from all of his students,' Romulus continued. 'And from what I hear your grades are slipping more and more these days.'

'Perhaps you're not cut out to attend one of the top schools in the country,' Remus taunted. 'Maybe you're just a fraud.'

That did it for Marc. He had studied hard and long to gain a place at the Institute. No newcomer was going to question his right to be there. He strode forward and grabbed Remus by the lapels of his smartly tailored jacket.

'No, Marc,' Rebecca said. 'Don't let them get to you: they're not worth it.'

Rebecca was right, and Marc knew it. Still it was with some reluctance that he let go of Remus. The twin made an exaggerated pretence at smoothing the imaginary creases in his jacket.

'Tut, tut, such aggression,' Remus sniggered. 'Perhaps it's *me* who should report *you* to the General. Falling grades and a bad attitude – I'm sure he wouldn't take kindly to that.'

'Get lost, creep,' Marc said angrily, and stormed past the twins, followed by Rebecca. The twins laughed as they watched them leave.

When they were outside, Marc punched his fist violently into the palm of his other hand. Rebecca looked at him in concern.

'Don't let those two get to you, Marc,' she said softly. 'Scumbags like that just aren't worth it.'

'They make me so angry, Bec,' he confided. 'They've only been here a couple of weeks and they're treating everyone like dirt. What makes them think that they're so superior to everyone else? What gives them the right to bully little kids like Peter?'

'It's not only Peter they've been upsetting,' Rebecca revealed. 'From what I hear they've been picking on some of the other kids as well.'

'Hasn't anyone told Axford?'

'Everyone's too frightened,' Rebecca told him. 'If they tell, then they're scared what the twins might do to them. Besides, Eva's taken something of a shine to them.'

'I bet they'd be capable of anything,' Marc said, and shuddered. 'They give me the creeps . . .'

'Who gives you the creeps?'

Marc and Rebecca turned around to see Joey walking up the driveway towards them. Before Marc could answer the question, Joey said, 'Don't tell me – the Twins from Hell, right?'

'How d'you know that?' Marc asked.

'Well, I could say I read your mind,' Joey chuckled, but before Marc could take him seriously, he added:

'But it's obvious, isn't it? When it comes to creepiness, those two guys wrote the book.'

'They're bullies as well,' Rebecca said. 'I hate that.'

'Don't I know it,' Joey said with feeling. 'They've been terrorising some guys in my math class. Everyone's real scared of them. I tell you, since those two turned up, the atmosphere at the Institute has changed for the worse, especially for the younger kids.'

'We should do something about it,' Rebecca decided, but Joey shook his head.

'Maybe so, but not now,' he said. 'I'm going off to Darkfell Rise.'

'I thought the Zarathustra concert wasn't for another three days,' Rebecca said.

'That's right,' Joey said, 'but they're starting to set up for the gig today. I figured that if I got friendly with the road crew then I might get a chance to go see the band backstage after the gig!'

'Hey, Joey, that isn't such a bad idea,' Marc said. 'You mind if I tag along?'

Rebecca lifted her hands up in despair. 'I do not believe I'm hearing this!' she said. 'You two are turning into a proper pair of groupies!'

'Students of serious music,' Marc insisted, with a smile. 'Say, Joey, do you think we might be able to get their autographs?'

'Marc, my man, I'd settle for just shaking hands with them,' Joey replied in all seriousness. 'I mean, those guys aren't just stars, they're like gods. I tell you, if I could give 'em five, then I'd never wash that hand again!'

'You two are impossible,' Rebecca laughed. 'I'm going off to the radio telescope. At least I can find some stars who really interest me, instead of a bunch of third-rate rockers!'

Dateline: The Darkfell Rise;
Wednesday 24 June; 18.23.

By the time Marc and Joey arrived at the Darkfell Rise dusk was falling, but the hill was still bustling with activity. Several vans and large lorries had been parked at the foot of the hill, and workmen were busy unloading the seating for the forthcoming concert.

At the top of the hill, and in clear sight of the Darkfell Ring, carpenters were assembling the massive stage area, and electricians were already fixing up overhead lights and the massive sound system. Even though the concert was still three days away there was a general air of anticipation and excitement. This, everyone seemed to agree, was going to be the major musical event of the decade.

'I can't wait,' Joey said, as they approached the stage area. 'Will you take a look at that sound system, for one thing!'

Marc studied the massive sets of speakers which had been placed on either side of the stage. About seven metres in height, connected to a central computer system at the foot of the stage, and twinkling with what seemed like a thousand differently coloured lights, they seemed to belong more in a science-fiction movie than a rock concert. He let out a long whistle of appreciation.

'I've never seen a PA system like that before,' he told Joey.

'Those muthas could blast you all the way to Mars and back,' Joey agreed. 'I bet they'll be able to hear it for miles around.'

'That'll really upset Miss Rumford,' Marc chuckled.

'Not to mention Rebecca,' Joey added wickedly.

'Yeah,' Marc agreed with a smile. He glanced back at the radio telescope in the distance. 'Rebecca doesn't know what she'll be missing. She's probably up there now, studying the stars.'

'Well, I know which stars I'm interested in,' Joey said, and then frowned as a surly-looking character with a heavy-metal T-shirt, scraggly long hair, and a potbelly swaggered up to them.

'What are you kids doing here?' the stranger drawled, his voice full of menace.

Joey, who might only have been thirteen but certainly didn't regard himself as a 'kid', glowered at the man. 'We're watching you set up for the Zarathustra gig,' he said defiantly. 'You got a problem with that?'

'Yeah. We don't want children running around and getting in the way.'

'We are not children,' Marc said. 'And you don't own the Darkfell Rise, you know.'

The man took a step towards them. It was looking as if things might turn nasty, when another man came up the hill to join them. The newcomer seemed to be in his late twenties. He was tall and slim with stylishly long raven-black hair and designer stubble. He was wearing a trendy – and obviously very expensive – casual suit.

'It's OK, Jim,' the newcomer said. There was a faint transatlantic burr to his voice. 'Let me deal with this.'

'Scott, we can't have these kids hanging around, especially not now –' Jim started to protest but Scott raised a hand to indicate that he should be quiet.

'Leave it, OK?' he said. 'Besides these aren't just any kids.' He smiled at Marc and Joey. 'You're students from the Institute, right?'

Marc and Joey exchanged puzzled looks. 'That's right,' Joey said. 'But how could you know?'

Scott smiled at Joey. 'You're from the States,' he said. 'There aren't that many American kids in sleepy old Brentmouth.' He turned to Marc and pointed out his trendy leather jacket, his scuffed-up Cats, his dyed-blond hair and the earring in his right ear. 'And you look and dress far too individually to be just a village kid. Am I right?'

Marc nodded and smiled. Rebecca was always telling him that he didn't dress smartly enough. It was nice to meet someone who appreciated his sense of style!

'The Institute is famous the world over,' Scott said. 'Institute students are . . . kind of special . . .'

'Hey, we're not that special,' Marc said, with fake modesty. 'Sure, we're a lot brighter than other kids, especially in the sciences, but –'

Scott cut him short. 'No,' he said firmly, 'you're *special*. Don't put yourselves down.'

Marc smiled. There was something very likeable about Scott. Scott waved Jim off and then turned back to the two boys. 'Sorry about Jim,' he said, and the look in his brilliantly blue eyes suggested that he was being genuine. 'He's not exactly well-known for his manners at the best of times, but he is a good roadie.'

'Are you a roadie as well?' Joey asked.

'Not exactly,' Scott replied with a smile.

'I know who you are!' Marc suddenly realised, and remembered reading an article in the *NME* several months ago. 'You're Scott Masters, the rock promoter! You're the guy who persuaded Zarathustra to get back together and do this concert.'

Scott beamed, obviously pleased that Marc knew who he was. Joey went up to the older man and shook his hand.

'Mr Masters –' he began.

'Scott,' Scott corrected him.

'Scott, you are the best ever!' he enthused. 'For the past ten years everyone's been trying to persuade Zarathustra to re-form, and then you pop out of nowhere and manage it! How did you pull that one off?'

Scott blushed at Joey's unreserved praise. 'Maybe I just tried a different approach to all the others,' he said modestly. 'Anyway the most important thing is that Zarathustra will be playing here on the Darkfell Rise, and people are coming from all over the country to see them.'

'It's going to be a great gig,' Joey agreed.

'And it's a fantastic location,' Scott said. He glanced

over at the standing stones in the distance and smiled to himself. 'The Darkfell Ring is really going to add to the atmosphere of the event.'

Joey grinned. 'Just don't let some of the villagers hear you say that,' he chuckled.

Scott sighed. 'I know there's been a lot of local opposition to the gig,' he said sadly. 'But trust me, there's absolutely nothing to worry about.'

'Oh no?' Marc said, and nodded over to the stage area. It seemed that the burly, mean-mouthed Jim had met his match. A fury in tweeds and waving a walking stick was giving him a very loud piece of her mind: Miss Olive Rumford had arrived. They watched as Jim pointed over to Scott and she marched over the hill towards them.

Marc smiled sheepishly at Miss Rumford, who gave him the sort of look which clearly suggested that she suspected him of colluding with the enemy. Then he introduced her to Scott.

Miss Rumford opened her mouth to speak and then saw Scott's face. Her breath caught in her throat, and her own face suddenly went pale.

'Do I know you, young man?' she asked.

Scott smiled his most engaging smile and shook his head. 'I doubt it, madam,' he said. 'I've never been here before in my life.'

'It's just that I thought . . . Oh, never mind,' she said. She regained her composure. 'I take it that you are the person responsible for this concert?' She indicated the stage and the rows of seating which were already being assembled.

Scott gave Marc and Joey a helpless look and then said that, yes, he was.

'Then you must call the whole thing off,' Miss Rumford said.

'I'm sorry, Miss Rumford,' Scott said, all politeness and charm. 'There are thousands of people coming. I can't call a concert off just like that.'

'Yeah, Miss Rumford, people have been waiting years for this gig,' Joey added. 'There'll be some major grief if it doesn't go ahead now.'

'The Darkfell Rise is sacred land,' Miss Rumford said, and Marc prayed that she wasn't going to bring up the subject of fairies again. Thankfully, she didn't, but continued, 'And then there's the problem of the disappearances.'

'Disappearances?' Scott said and there was a faint trace of a smile around his lips. 'Now that is interesting.'

Miss Rumford harrumphed with satisfaction: at last someone in Brentmouth who saw good sense! She turned to Marc and Joey.

'At last, someone who's taking me seriously!' she said. 'Then you will call off the concert, Mr Masters?'

Scott shook his head. 'Of course I won't,' he told her. 'But maybe I could use this legend for some extra publicity . . .'

'What do you mean?' asked Marc.

'Maybe I could get some T-shirts made up,' he said. 'You know the sort of thing: "I Escaped The Darkfell Ring". It'd be great PR for the gig.'

Miss Rumford exploded and waved her walking

stick angrily at Scott, who sensibly took a step back. 'How dare you, young man!' she cried. 'How dare you treat with contempt all that my ancestors have held sacred for centuries?'

'Your ancestors?' Scott asked urgently.

'Yes, there have been Rumfords living here in the village since anyone can remember,' she told him.

'How long for?' Scott asked, suddenly very interested indeed.

'Since the time of the Conqueror at least, and we have always stuck to our principles,' she replied. 'And I shall stop this damnable concert going ahead on the Darkfell Rise if it's the last thing I do!'

'I'm afraid you can't, Miss Rumford,' Scott said calmly.

'Can't? Of course I can!' Miss Rumford said. By now her entire body was shaking with rage. 'I shall see General Axford the first thing in the morning. He's a respected leader of our community. If anyone can help me, it will be him.'

'Somehow I don't think you'll succeed,' Scott told her, and Miss Rumford shook even more. Whether it was with anger this time, or down to Scott's calm and superior attitude, Marc and Joey found it difficult to tell.

'If it's a battle you want, then it's a battle you'll get,' Miss Rumford declared furiously, and turned sharply around and stormed off back down the hill.

When she had gone, Scott ran his fingers through his hair and let out a long whistle. 'Are all the locals like that?' he asked Marc and Joey, who both grinned.

'Nah,' Joey said, 'some of them are even nuttier.'

Marc stared thoughtfully after the departing form of Miss Rumford. 'I've never seen her so angry before,' he told them. 'Stopping this gig must be really important to her.'

'Maybe she just doesn't want her fairy friends disturbed,' joked Joey, and then he turned back to the stones of the Darkfell Ring.

There was no doubt about it now. The stones were glowing with a faint, unearthly light. Yet, even as he watched, the light faded, until the stones returned to the same dull grey colour they had been for centuries.

And then Joey casually looked up into the night-time sky at a thin, pale streak of light in the blackness, barely visible to the naked eye. Even Joey, with his heightened senses, thought nothing about it as he and Marc headed off down the hill.

As far as he was concerned, one comet was pretty much the same as any other.

Dateline: Fetch Hill Radio Telescope;
Wednesday 24 June; 19.00.

Rebecca was looking through the readings which were coming out of the computer. The radio telescope was trained, as ever, on the approaching Comet Zarathustra, and she frowned as she checked and double-checked the read-outs. Then, being Rebecca, she triple-checked them.

Yes, there was no doubt about it, the pulses given out by the comet were getting stronger and stronger. For one crazy moment she thought that it was signalling or sending a message to something or someone, calling out across the blackness of space to the planet Earth.

And then she dismissed the idea from her mind.

After all, that was impossible. That sort of thing only happened on low-budget movies and late-night TV shows.

Didn't it?

THE PSYCHIC ZONE

9

A Missed Meeting

Dateline: The Darkfell Rise;
Thursday 25 June; 12.42.

The following day, Joey was whistling happily to himself as he walked up the side of the Darkfell Rise where Scott was making last-minute arrangements for tomorrow's concert.

The stage area was now almost ready, and electricians were busy fixing up the overhead lights. People carrying clipboards and mobile phones were trying to decide the best place to set up the TV cameras. The Zarathustra concert was due to be televised live all over the world, and – if the reports in this morning's breakfast TV had been true – the excitement was going to be enormous.

Joey glanced over at the Darkfell Ring. In the morning sun the stones looked unthreatening, and he wondered how he and Marc could have been so dim to have let themselves get fazed by them. Boy, had they ever been a couple of prize wusses! How could anyone get freaked out by an empty ring of standing stones?

Empty?

Joey shaded his eyes from the sun and looked again. There were now three figures standing in the centre of the Darkfell Ring. He could have sworn that they hadn't been there just a few seconds ago. Or had he simply not noticed them? He squinted his eyes to take a closer look.

Two of the people he recognised as Romulus and Remus, and Joey wondered what business they had up on the Darkfell Rise.

Then he realised exactly what the two boys were up to. They were advancing threateningly on the third person in the ring, who was partly obscured by one of the larger stones.

It was obvious what had happened. Romulus and Remus had lured one of the younger kids from the Institute up to the Ring. He saw one of the twins raise his arm to strike the third person, who yelped in fear.

And do they ever have a fight on their hands! Joey thought. He clenched his fists and started running up towards the Ring. He'd flattened guys twice their size back home in Harlem, and the twins weren't going to pose him any problems at all!

As he approached the stones, his heart sank as he recognised the other person in the Ring. It was Colette. He could see the frightened look on her face beneath her dark glasses. He put on an extra spurt of speed.

'Get your filthy hands off her, you creeps!'

The twins and Colette turned around to see him racing up towards them. There was a sly smile on the faces of Romulus and Remus which made Joey even more angry.

'Well, well, well, if it isn't that little slum kid,' Remus said.

Joey saw red. He launched himself on the twin who had made the derogatory remark. He headbutted him in the stomach and knocked him down to the ground, where he started to pummel him with his fists.

'I'll teach you to bully defenceless girls!'

The two of them rolled around on the barren ground within the Darkfell Ring. Joey was so angry that he never paused to wonder why Remus was making no effort to defend himself, or why Romulus was standing there watching them and not trying to help his brother.

'Stop it!' Colette cried out. 'Leave him alone, Joey!'

Remus took advantage of the distraction. He pushed Joey off him and stood up. Just as before, when Marc had threatened his brother, the twin made an exaggerated show of smoothing the creases of his lapels.

Joey looked in amazement at Colette. 'Colette, I've just gone and rescued you from these two jerks!'

'Maybe I didn't need rescuing,' Colette said, her voice rising in anger as well. 'I can look after myself perfectly well, you know!'

'But they were ganging up on you!' he protested. 'I saw them hit you!'

'You saw nothing of the sort,' Colette said. 'Romulus and Remus are friends of mine.'

'These scuzzballs?' he asked in disbelief.

Romulus chuckled. Remus sneered.

'I met them down in the village a few days ago,' Colette said. 'We're getting on really well. We're all going to the concert tomorrow.'

This was too much for Joey to believe, and he didn't know which way to turn. He looked at the twins. They were grinning and staring superiorly at him with those weird eyes of theirs. Then he glanced back at Colette.

'So just leave me alone, will you?' she said flatly.

The twins laughed at Joey's dismay and then turned back to Colette. 'We're off back to the Institute,' they told her. 'Will we see you later?'

'Of course,' Colette said. 'I'm seeing Rebecca at Fetch Hill at one. She's promised to lend me one of her magazines.'

'One o'clock?' Joey asked and looked at his watch. It was almost twelve fifty-five now, and Fetch Hill was a good thirty minutes' walk away. 'You'll be late.'

Colette looked scornfully at him. 'No, I won't,' she claimed. 'I'll get a cab.' She turned back to the twins. 'We can meet up with each other after that.'

The twins nodded in agreement and then walked off down the hill, although not without glancing spitefully back at Joey. When they had left, Joey turned to Colette.

'I can't believe you sticking up for those louses, Colette!' he exploded. 'They're the worst kind of bullies there are. All the young kids back at the

Institute are scared senseless of them!'

'Which just goes to show how stupid people at the Institute can be,' Colette said.

'That's wrong and you know it,' Joey said, as he bridled at the insult. 'Those two guys are bad news, Colette.'

Colette looked angrily at Joey. 'Let me choose my own friends, OK?' she said.

'But –'

'I said leave me alone, OK!' Colette snapped back.

Joey shrugged his shoulders. If Colette was going to behave like a little fool when all he was doing was trying to look after her, then that was her business, he decided.

'Suit yourself,' he said finally.

'I will,' Colette said, and turned to go. As she made her way down the hill in the direction that the twins had taken, there was a faint smile on her lips. It was a smile which, if Joey had seen it, would have chilled him to the bone.

'Lovers' tiff?' asked a familiar voice behind Joey, and he turned around. Scott was there, all smiles as usual.

Joey smiled weakly at the rock promoter. 'No,' he said. 'Things were just getting a little heated between us, that's all.' He shook his head sadly. 'Y' know something, Scott? I reckon even if I live to be thirty I'm never gonna understand women!'

Scott laughed. 'We men aren't supposed to!' he joked. 'Say, did you see what I saw just now?'

Joey frowned, and asked Scott what he meant. Scott

pointed to the stones of the Darkfell Ring.

'I guess it must have just been a trick of the light,' he said, 'but I could have sworn I saw those stones glow.'

Joey shuddered; it had suddenly turned very cold indeed.

'Still, I suppose it must have been my imagination,' Scott reasoned. 'Now, c'mon, Joey, I thought you were coming here to help me set up the gig for tomorrow. Everything's got to be perfect for the most intense, most happening event this part of the world has ever seen. I tell you, my friend, tomorrow night is going to be one hell of a night to remember!'

Joey left the Ring and walked down the Darkfell Rise to the stage area, unaware that they were both being watched.

Behind a stone, one of the Demons of the Darkfell Ring chittered happily to itself. Yes, everything would certainly be perfect. They had all made sure of that. Hundreds of minds, youthful, vibrant and alive. Ready for feasting upon. Hundreds of new bodies, just fit for the taking.

And yes, Scott had been right. Tomorrow would indeed be one hell of a night to remember.

If, of course, there was anyone left alive to remember.

CHANGELINGS

'I've never been so disappointed in my life,' Miss Rumford said as she was escorted out of General Axford's office by Eva. The younger woman stared down through her dark glasses with obvious contempt for the older woman.

'I'm terribly sorry that your journey here has been a wasted one,' Eva said. She didn't sound the least bit sorry.

'I was supposed to be meeting General Axford here, young lady,' Miss Rumford reminded her frostily. 'I have never known him to break an appointment before without prior notice. A gentleman of the old school, he is.'

'He's been called down to London urgently,' Eva informed her once again. 'He told me to reschedule your meeting. Perhaps in three days' time?'

Miss Rumford snorted with disdain. 'Three days will be three days too late,' she said. 'This damnable rock festival will have gone ahead and happened by then.'

'Then I'm sorry, but there's nothing else that I can do for you,' Eva said. She smiled her most insincere smile. 'I have urgent business to attend to now. Please show yourself out.'

Eva walked back into the office and slammed shut the door in Miss Rumford's face, leaving the older woman fuming in the corridor. Resigning herself to the fact that there was no way she was going to stop the rock concert, she started to head for the main exit, when Marc came out of one of the classrooms.

'Hi, there, Miss Rumford,' he said cheerily, and frowned when he saw the angry look on her face. She told him what had happened in Axford's office.

'Yeah, that is unusual of old Axford,' Marc agreed. 'No matter what his faults are, he's always been a stickler for manners and time-keeping. I guess that's what comes from having served in the army all those years ago.'

'Exactly who is that woman?' Miss Rumford asked, referring to Eva. Marc told her that she was Axford's personal assistant.

'I know that. But where does she come from? What is she?'

'How do you mean, Miss Rumford?' Marc asked.

Miss Rumford shrugged her shoulders. 'I'm not quite sure,' she said. 'But she seems so cold . . . unnaturally so . . .'

'We call her the "Ice Queen" when we think she's not listening,' Marc said lightly, even though he too had always had some doubts about Eva's true identity. 'Trouble is, it seems that she always is listening!'

'She said that the General had been called away to London to attend some ministerial meeting.'

'I guess that's possible,' Marc said. 'The politicos down in London are always arguing about the size of the Institute's grant.'

'With Sergeant Ashby gone, the General was the only one who could have raised enough local opposition to halt the concert,' she told him.

'C'mon, Miss Rumford,' Marc said reasonably. 'It's only a rock concert after all.'

Miss Rumford stared at Marc in disbelief. 'It is blasphemy,' she declared. 'To our ancestors the stones were sacred. To use them for any other reason would be inviting the forces of evil to descend on us all.'

Marc smiled. 'Don't you think you're taking things too far, Miss Rumford?' he asked gently. 'It's only a rock concert after all.'

Miss Rumford glared at him. 'I am a white witch,' she reminded him. 'I feel things more than others. Understand things more. See more deeply than anyone at the Institute. And I tell you, the forces of darkness are readying themselves for an assault. The stones of the Darkfell Ring must not be defiled by these . . . these . . . these teenyboppers!'

Marc winced at Miss Rumford's outdated language. 'I'm sure Scott wouldn't want to upset anyone's religious beliefs,' he reassured her. 'Maybe if you had another word with him? He seems an OK sort of guy.'

Miss Rumford's face darkened. 'Ah, yes, the young – the *very* young – Scott Masters, the man behind the concert. If that is who he really is, of course . . .'

'What do you mean?' Marc asked.

Miss Rumford regarded Marc carefully for a moment through her tiny *pince-nez* spectacles. 'Can I trust you?'

Marc frowned, not quite understanding what she meant but finally said that, yes, she could.

Miss Rumford nodded wisely. 'Yes, I thought so,' she said. 'I can sense that you're not like the other scientists at the Institute. That you believe in things for which there is as yet no scientific proof.'

'I've an open mind, that's all,' Marc said and hoped that Miss Rumford wasn't going to turn the subject round to fairies and changelings again.

'People laugh at me behind my back here in Brentmouth,' Miss Rumford began and, when Marc protested, said, 'Don't contradict me, my boy, I know they do. "Batty old Rumford", they call me, when I talk about the Little Folk and the disappearances around the Darkfell Ring . . .'

'You have to admit that believing in fairy abductions is a little unusual for this day and age,' Marc said, as tactfully as he could.

'So what happened to your missing passengers on board that aircraft?' Miss Rumford asked.

'The twins didn't take the plane in the end,' Marc told her, and then added rather uncharitably: 'although I wish that they had done. They've caused nothing but bad feeling at the Institute with their bullying ways.'

'And what happened to the pilot of the plane?' she asked. 'Planes don't fly by themselves, you know. There is evil about, Marc, I know it.'

Marc smiled indulgently at Miss Rumford. 'Now how can you know that?' he asked.

'Come to my house, Rowan Cottage, later this afternoon,' she said. 'There's something I want to show you.'

'I was supposed to be seeing Joey,' Marc said.

'This is important, young man,' Miss Rumford insisted.

Marc shrugged his shoulders. He guessed that he could put Joey off. He promised that he'd come around later.

'I'm sorry you didn't get to see the General, Miss Rumford,' he said, before he left.

'I just hope that Mr John Smith is pleased with himself.'

'Who?'

'John Smith,' Miss Rumford repeated, not understanding why Marc had suddenly gone very pale indeed. 'That was who called the General down to London so suddenly. Or at least that's what that woman told me. Do you know the man?'

'Er . . . no,' Marc lied. Could this have been the same man who had told them not to investigate the mystery of the missing aircraft? And was it also the same John Smith who had arranged for the police sergeant's transfer down to London? Marc was sure that it was.

'Whoever he is, he's the man who's finally guaranteed that the concert will go ahead,' Miss Rumford said and stormed off down the corridor.

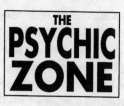

THE PSYCHIC ZONE

10

The Lodestone

Dateline: Fetch Hill Radio Telescope;
Thursday 25 June; 13.05.

Rebecca was alone in the control room when someone sneaked up behind her and placed their hands over her eyes. She screamed in panic and leapt up to see who had crept up on her as silently as a cat hunting down its prey.

'Colette, you startled me!' she said, and the younger girl just grinned at her practical joke.

'You hadn't forgotten our lunch date?' she asked. 'You said that you'd lend me that magazine of yours and then we'd go down into the village and try out that trendy new cappuccino bar.'

'Of course I hadn't,' Rebecca said.

She started to search amongst the papers and computer read-outs on the desk for the magazine she'd promised Colette. It was buried somewhere there, she knew. Unfortunately, Rebecca's precise and analytical mind didn't quite extend to tidy desks.

Suddenly an eminently sensible thought struck Rebecca and she stopped looking for a second. She stared past Colette and towards the closed door of the control room.

'How did you get in here?' she asked. Colette frowned.

'Through the door,' she said, and then asked, 'Did you think I walked through the walls?'

Rebecca chose not to ask why Colette was being so unusually flippant. Instead she left her desk and started to walk over to the door.

'I could have sworn it was locked,' she said, and Colette stopped her.

'Locked? You mean Professor Henderson locks you in here?' she asked in disbelief. 'I thought you chose to come here in your free periods. I didn't think it was a punishment!'

Rebecca laughed. 'The rest of the Prof's staff are out at lunch, but I wanted to stay until you arrived. There's lots of valuable equipment here, and officially I'm not supposed to be left on my own. So they gave me the key to lock myself in.'

She reached over and turned the door handle. No doubt about it, it was locked.

'That's impossible,' Colette said. She tried the door herself. There was a slight click of tumblers and it opened easily. 'It was probably only jammed when you tried it.'

'I must have forgotten to lock it after all,' she said. 'Come on, Colette, let's go and hit that cappuccino bar before Miss Rumford decides that it's an example of all that's decadent in sleepy old Brentmouth and tries to close it down!'

'Aren't you forgetting something?' Colette asked. She nodded back at Rebecca's untidy desk. 'That magazine you promised me.'

'Of course,' Rebecca said. While she rummaged around her papers, Colette examined some of the equipment and computing machines which lined the wall of the control room. She idly played around with some of the dials and touch-sensitive controls. A few lights started to flicker. The digital read-outs on some of the computer LEDs altered slightly.

'Here! I've found it!' Rebecca said and pulled out the magazine she'd been looking for. The title read *Cosmological Review*. It was a new periodical from the States which Rebecca's scientist mother received on subscription. She handed the magazine over to Colette.

'Thanks, I'll give it back to you tomorrow,' Colette promised.

'Keep it for as long as you want,' Rebecca told her. 'Although I'm surprised that you'd be interested in something like this.'

Colette stopped flicking through the pages, and looked up. There was a slightly embarrassed look on her face.

'I just felt so silly the other night when Marc and Joey were teasing me,' she said awkwardly. 'I thought I'd better show that I'm not as stupid as they think, even though I don't attend the Institute.'

'No one thinks you're stupid, Colette,' Rebecca said with a puzzled smile. Colette had never expressed these kinds of feelings before.

She glanced at the page Colette was reading. It was a report on the approaching comet and was accompanied by a series of scientific equations which tried to define the comet's weight, size and distance from Earth.

'Is this all that you scientists have found out about the comet?' Colette asked.

'Almost everything,' she told her. Colette looked interested.

'What do you mean?'

Rebecca opened the drawer to her desk and pulled out sheets of computer print-out. She pointed out the jagged lines on several of the graphs.

'What are they?' Colette asked.

Rebecca shrugged her shoulders. 'If I didn't know any better, I'd say they were regular radio emissions,' she told her. 'See how the lines reach a peak every few centimetres and then drop right down again. A regular pattern repeated over and over again.'

'There must be something wrong with the telescope,' Colette said, and rammed the copy of *Cosmological Review* into her backpack.

'I know,' Rebecca said. 'Otherwise why hasn't any other radio telescope in the world picked up on it?'

'Unless it's all part of an international cover-up!' Colette joked.

'Now you sound like Marc!' Rebecca said.

'I wish he was coming with us for lunch,' Colette

said, suddenly her old wistful self again. Rebecca smiled to herself. She had often suspected the younger girl of having something of a crush on her best friend.

'He's due over at Miss Rumford's at two-thirty,' Rebecca told her.

'What for?' Colette's voice was urgent now.

'Some old mumbo-jumbo, no doubt,' Rebecca said. 'I'm glad you're finally taking an interest in science, 'cos our Marc seems to be heading on a one-way ticket to La-La-Land! Now come on, Colette! Those cappuccinos and cream cakes won't last forever!'

Dateline: Rowan Cottage;
Thursday 25 June; 14.25.

Rowan Cottage was tiny and ramshackle, and nestled in a sleepy dell just a little way off from the main village of Brentmouth, but within sight of the Darkfell Rise to the west and the Fetch Hill Radio Telescope to the east.

Ivy scrambled up the walls on either side of the front door. Chintz curtains were drawn over small, dimpled windows. A thin trail of smoke came from the chimney on top of the thatched roof.

Rowan Cottage seemed somehow timeless, a place where little had changed in hundreds of years. It reminded Marc of the sort of homes he'd only ever seen before depicted on the front of biscuit-tin boxes. To call it quaint would be to make it sound more well-kept than it really was. But to call it run-down would be to deny the definite charm which hung about the house.

Before Marc could reach for the knocker, the door opened. Miss Rumford popped out her head and looked this way and that before ushering Marc inside. Marc smiled.

'What's the big secret, Miss Rumford?' Marc asked as the old woman showed him into her small parlour where a pot of tea and two cups were waiting for them on a table.

Marc looked around him. An old Welsh dresser in the corner of the room displayed fine crockery, tiny china figures and strange wooden charms. Several paintings hung on the otherwise plain, white-washed walls. Judging by the resemblance, Marc guessed that they had to be some of Miss Rumford's relatives – perhaps even some of the white witches who she had said had lived here since anyone could ever remember.

A small set of banners were leaning against one wall. Marc read the words painted on them. *Popsters Go Home!* they read. **Hands Off Our Holy Stones!** It seemed that, even without General Axford's help, Miss Rumford had successfully organised the villagers into resistance against the forthcoming Zarathustra concert. Scott was due some pretty formidable opposition on the day of the concert.

The facing wall was completely lined by book-shelves creaking under the weight of volumes which appeared to be hundreds of years old. As Miss Rumford poured the tea, Marc read the titles on some of the spines: *Witchcraft Today*; *The Standing Stones of England and Ireland*; *The Fairy Faith*; and then, strangest of all: *Cosmological Review*.

Marc took the magazine down and was about to quiz Miss Rumford over its presence on her shelves when the old woman offered him a cup. He put down the review and sipped at his tea. It was sweet and hot.

'So what's the big secret, Miss Rumford?' Marc repeated his question, and peered over the rim of his teacup at the white witch. 'What is it that you want to show me?'

Miss Rumford got up from the table and walked over to the dresser. 'My family have lived here for as long as anyone can remember,' she said and pulled open the drawer. Marc saw her take something out and hide it in the palm of her hand.

'Yes, you told me that,' Marc reminded her. He watched as she took an old leather-bound scrapbook from one of the bookshelves and then returned to the table. She sat down and peered at Marc through wise, all-seeing eyes. But was it Marc's imagination or was there fear in those eyes as well?

'From generation to generation my family have passed down tales of the old times,' she said in a hushed voice. 'But things other than tales can be passed down the centuries.'

Miss Rumford opened up her hand to let Marc see what she had been concealing.

It was a small, flat stone, roughly circular in shape, with a strange design etched into its grey-white surface. Marc peered at the pattern: several dots linked to each other by straight lines. It appeared vaguely familiar, and he wondered where he had seen the design before.

'What is it? Some sort of talisman or lucky charm?' It reminded him of the magic amulets he'd seen on late-night fantasy movies on the Sci-Fi Channel. Miss Rumford handed it to him and he weighted it in his hand. It felt much heavier than something its size should have done.

'We Rumfords call it the Lodestone,' she told him, 'and it has always been in our family.'

'Lodestone?'

'No one knows why it's called that,' Miss Rumford admitted. By now her voice had lowered itself to a whisper and Marc had to lean forwards to hear her. 'Just as we don't know how it came into my family's possession in the first place.'

'Well, I suppose it looks kind of interesting,' Marc said. He casually threw it up into the air, and then caught it in the palm of his hand. 'But what's so special about it?'

Miss Rumford looked around her as if to check that no one was listening in to their conversation.

'*They* want it back,' she told him in hushed tones. 'The Old Ones want it back.'

Marc sat back in his chair and looked strangely at Miss Rumford. Maybe Rebecca had been right, he reflected. Maybe Miss Rumford really was as nutty as a fruitcake, after all.

'Er . . . how can you know that?' he asked, trying unsuccessfully to hide the doubt in his voice.

'The burglaries around Brentmouth, of course,' she told him. 'They've been breaking into houses, searching for the Lodestone.'

Marc sighed. 'These burglaries have been the work of local kids,' he told her. 'Anyway, that's what old Ashby used to say.'

Miss Rumford laughed scornfully. 'Then why have none of them been caught?' she asked.

'Sergeant Ashby wasn't exactly Sherlock Holmes,' Marc said with a smile. 'He couldn't even catch a cold, let alone a thief! Anyway, which self-respecting young housebreaker would want to get their hands on an old lump of rock?'

'Some people call the stones of the Darkfell Ring old lumps of rock, and we both know that they are much more than that,' she told him and then sadly hung her head. 'But I see that I am wasting my time with you. You're like all the rest at the Institute. Your scientific education is blinkering you to what's under your noses.'

'I'm sorry, Miss Rumford.' He meant it.

'The Lodestone *glows*,' Miss Rumford said dramatically. 'Ever since the rock concert was announced it has shone with a weird, unearthly light. It's an omen, an omen of evil things to come.'

Marc looked at the piece of stone in his hand. For a second he thought that the room seemed to have become colder.

'Well, it's not glowing now,' he said, trying hard not to upset the old woman's feelings.

He needn't have bothered. Miss Rumford snatched

the stone from him and slammed it down on to the table, next to the leather-bound scrapbook she'd taken from the shelf.

'I thought I could trust you!' she said angrily.

'Sure, I'd like to believe you,' Marc claimed.

'Then perhaps this will convince you that all is not as it should be in the village of Brentmouth!' Miss Rumford said. She pushed the scrapbook in Marc's direction.

He opened it up. The volume smelt old and musty, and Marc guessed that Miss Rumford must have owned it for some thirty or forty years. He was proved correct when he read the date on some of the faded and yellowed newspaper cuttings. Most of them came from the 1960s, when Miss Rumford had been a young woman, living with her parents at Rowan Cottage.

He turned to the page Miss Rumford indicated. Pasted down were two small clippings from the local newspaper of the time. One announced the engagement of one Seth Murray to Miss Olive Elizabeth Rumford.

'They're your wedding banns. I heard about your being dumped all those years ago,' Marc said, and then apologised for his lack of tact. 'Whoops. Sorry, my foot always seems to end up in my mouth.'

To his surprise Miss Rumford wasn't annoyed. She told him to look at the second cutting.

It was a brief report on the disappearance of Seth Murray, just a few days before his wedding was due to take place. Seth had been expected at the next-but-one village to organise the entertainment for the wedding reception, but had never turned up.

The last anyone had ever seen him, he'd been spotted heading towards the Darkfell Rise. His fiancée was distraught, the newspaper reported. At the bottom of the article there was a small photograph of the missing man.

'They never found him,' Miss Rumford remembered sadly. 'So the gossips around here said that he'd – as you so eloquently put it – "dumped me".'

'But didn't the police –'

Miss Rumford shook her head. 'They said that there wasn't a case to investigate,' she remembered. 'Back in the sixties in Brentmouth we never asked questions. We accepted that. Especially when the Men in Black Suits came up from London to tell us so.'

'But what has your fiancé's disappearance to do with the Lodestone?' Marc asked, although he knew what the answer would be. Miss Rumford clearly believed that Seth Murray had been kidnapped by the Demons that lived within the Darkfell Ring.

'Take a look at his photograph more closely.'

Marc examined Seth Murray's picture again. The photograph had become faded over the years, but there was no doubt that Seth had been a handsome man in his time. He had thick, raven-black hair, a firm, determined jaw, and eyes which, even in the black-and-white photograph, were striking.

'He was a very good-looking man,' Marc told Miss Rumford. 'You must miss him a helluva lot – I mean, a great deal.'

'Look again.'

Deciding it would be better to humour her, Marc did as he was told. He frowned. There was something oddly familiar about Seth's face.

And then he knew whose picture he was looking at. He glanced up at Miss Rumford, who was nodding her head. He remembered the look of shock on her face when she'd first met Scott Masters on the Darkfell Rise.

'That's right,' she said. 'That man responsible for the rock concert is my fiancé: Seth Murray, who's been missing for almost thirty-five years!'

Marc shook his head. 'That's impossible!' he said. 'Scott is hardly in his thirties. If your fiancé was alive now then he'd be almost seventy.'

'You don't believe the evidence of your own eyes?' Miss Rumford asked a little sarcastically now. 'I thought that was the scientific way?'

Marc stood up to go. Humouring the old woman was one thing, but this was too much even for him.

'I'm sorry, Miss Rumford, but you can't be right. Look, you've been under a lot of strain recently, trying to get the Zarathustra gig cancelled. Maybe you need a rest.'

It was the red rag to the bull. No one had ever dared to tell Olive Rumford before that she needed a rest.

'Are you suggesting that I am mad, young man?' Miss Rumford boomed angrily. 'That I am getting senile?'

'No, I'm just –'

'Because if you are –'

Marc raised up his two hands in a calming gesture.

'Scott can't be Seth, Miss Rumford,' he repeated, much more forcibly this time. 'Face the facts. Whatever happened to Seth Murray you'll never see him again. He's probably dead by now.'

'No! Never!' Miss Rumford said. Her face reddened with rage and her whole body started to shake.

Marc took a step back. He was about to leave when something on the table caught his eye. He glanced back at Miss Rumford, and then returned his eyes to the Lodestone on the table.

'Now do you believe me?' Olive Rumford asked triumphantly. 'Now do you see that I'm telling the truth?'

The Lodestone was glowing faintly now. The lines linking the dots on its face pulsed with an eerie green light. It was a light that sent shivers down Marc's spine.

He reached out and picked up the stone. It tingled in the palm of his hand. Yet, even as he examined it more closely, the light faded, until it was once again just a lump of old stone with a strangely familiar pattern etched on to its surface.

'Miss Rumford, can I take this back to the Institute? I'd like to do some tests on it.'

'Tests? What sort of tests?'

'A spectrograph analysis,' he told her. When he was greeted with a look of blank incomprehension, he added: 'it'll tell us what this thing's made of.'

'All of your scientific research won't tell you what the Lodestone really is,' she sneered. 'The Lodestone is ancient and mystical, far older than your science. My mother and her mother before her guarded it, told me that it was a great treasure belonging to the creatures that live within the Darkfell Ring, that there was nothing they'd like more than to have it back. And if that were to happen then all the forces of evil within the Ring would be unleashed.'

'Yeah, that's right,' Marc said. He was glad Rebecca wasn't here now. She would have found it difficult not to scoff at Miss Rumford's beliefs.

'The Lodestone is not of our world of mortals,' Miss Rumford continued. 'It belongs to the Old Folk, the people who lived amongst the stones of the Darkfell Ring before history began.' She pulled back the chintz curtains and told Marc to look out through the dimpled window at the Darkfell Rise.

It was mid-afternoon now and the day was bright and summery. Yet there was something strange about the stones of the Darkfell Ring standing in the distance.

Surely they weren't glowing again, Marc wondered. Glowing just like the Lodestone had done, in fact.

Instinctively, he turned around to take another look at the Lodestone. It remained dull and lifeless. Just another lump of old rock.

And then Marc looked back at the Darkfell Ring. The stones were dark now, silhouetted in the sun. He could just make out the contractors' vehicles winding up the Rise to deliver more stage equipment for the forthcoming Zarathustra concert. They certainly hadn't noticed anything unusual about the stones. It must just have been a trick of the light, he reasoned.

After all, what possible connection could the Lodestone have with the six standing stones on the Darkfell Rise?

Unless, of course, Miss Rumford was right, and the Demons of the Darkfell Ring wanted it back . . .

THE PSYCHIC ZONE

11

Feelings Running High

Dateline: The Darkfell Rise;
Thursday 25 June; 17.23.

'Are you sure you want to help me with this gig?'

'Sure I do, Scott,' Marc said enthusiastically.

'What about your schoolwork?' Scott said. They were both sitting inside Scott's tiny motor-caravan which had been parked at the foot of the Rise. It was untidy and disorganised and, in its own way, just as ramshackle as Rowan Cottage.

'Hey, I'm way ahead on coursework,' Marc said (which wasn't strictly true). 'Anyway, half of my lecturers are going to the gig as well. And as for the others, I could tell them that helping out with the stage lights is good practical experience in physics, or electronics, or . . .'

Scott faced him with a knowing smile. 'And your suddenly unchecked enthusiasm has nothing to do with the fact that you want to meet Zarathustra as well, I guess?'

Marc lowered his head so that he couldn't see Scott's accusing eyes. 'Ah well . . . there is that, of course . . .'

Scott laughed and slapped Marc on the back. 'You wouldn't believe how many of the village kids have come up here asking for a job. Autograph hunters. People who want to sell stories to the Sunday papers. I said no to every single one of them.'

Marc shrugged his shoulders. 'You're letting Joey help you though,' he reminded him. When he'd arrived at Darkfell Rise, he'd spotted Joey by the stage explaining some of the finer points of computer programming to the sound technicians there. They'd looked suitably impressed, Marc had thought with a smile.

'I said no to all the village kids,' Scott corrected him. 'If *you* want to help us out then there's no problem.'

Marc brightened up. 'You mean it?' he asked. 'Scott, that's terrific! I can't wait to meet Zarathustra. But why me and Joey and no one else?'

'Zarathustra might be one of the biggest bands ever, but they've also had something of an image problem,' Scott admitted candidly. 'Some people said their music was only fit for layabouts, no hopers and scroungers off the State.'

'So the more of us from the Institute who turn up, the better it is for Zarathustra,' Marc realised.

'What other reason could there be?' Scott said with

a knowing smile. 'That's why there's free entrance to all Institute students on the day of the gig.'

'That's a great idea,' Marc agreed.

'It wasn't entirely mine,' Scott said modestly. 'But this way I'm sure they'll all come.'

'Not everyone,' Marc said. 'You haven't met Rebecca yet!'

'The girl who thinks Zarathustra are a bunch of talentless forty-somethings?' Scott asked with a smile. 'I'm sure she'll be much happier up at Fetch Hill with her very own Zarathustra. Although what she can see in a dirty snowball zooming around the galaxies I'll never understand.'

'Comets don't zoom around the galaxies, as you put it,' Marc chuckled. 'Just the solar system.'

'Of course,' Scott said and turned away from Marc.

Scott looked towards the stones of the Darkfell Ring. In two days' time the whole hill would be crowded with hundreds of thousands of people. Hundreds of thousands of eyes would be focused on the stage. Even now, the press was almost red-hot with excitement.

There'd even been a feature in last month's *Face* about the new state-of-the-art sound equipment which was to be tried out for the first time at the gig. The writer of the piece had admitted that she'd never seen anything like it before in her life. She had wondered what effect it would have on the band's music. Whatever it was, it was bound to be huge.

Scott turned back to Marc. There was an elated look on his face. 'I can hardly wait, Marc,' he told him confidentially. 'I've worked to get Zarathustra back

together for most of my life. And now to see it actually
happen! It's unbelievable.'

'How long have you been trying?'

'Ten years. Ever since I graduated from high school
and became a rock promoter.'

Marc did a rapid calculation in his head. 'So that
means you must be in your late twenties?'

Scott looked curiously at him. 'I turned thirty last
year,' he told Marc. 'Why so interested in my age?'

'No reason,' Marc lied. He joined Scott by the
window and looked out at the Darkfell Ring. 'It's a
great venue for the gig. I'm surprised you knew about
its existence. Unless you come from around here
originally.'

'What is all this? Twenty questions?' Scott asked.
There was now a slightly hard edge to his voice, as if
Marc was beginning to annoy him with his persistent
questioning. As if there was something he didn't want
Marc to know about.

'No,' Marc said guiltily. 'It's just that someone
down in the village wondered if you had ever been
her – I mean, whether you had any family around here.
She said you reminded her of someone. She seemed
to be really interested in you.'

'I'm flattered,' Scott said and then shared a conspi-
ratorial, all-lads-together look with Marc. 'And who
is she? I suppose it's too much to hope for that she's
young and good-looking?'

Marc shook his head. 'Sorry, you lucked out on that,
Scott,' he said good-naturedly. 'It's only Miss Rumford
down at Rowan Cottage.'

'Maybe she wants me to be her toy-boy,' Scott laughed and then dismissed the matter. He headed towards the door of the caravan. 'Now, come on, Marc, you can help me on stage.'

As Marc followed him to the door he noticed a pile of magazines scattered on the floor. They were the sort which he imagined anyone in the rock business would buy: the *NME*; *Smash Hits*; *MixMaster*; and one other familiar title.

'I thought you said that you weren't interested in comets,' Marc said and held up the latest edition of *Cosmological Review*, the one with the photograph of Comet Zarathustra on the cover.

'I'm not,' Scott said. 'But as the comet's supposed to be nearest to Earth on the night of the Zarathustra gig, I thought I'd do a little research into it.'

'You mean, make it a publicity gimmick?'

'Sure,' Scott said, and took the magazine from Marc and tossed it to the floor. He headed for the door. 'The more people who get to hear about this gig the better!'

'You might just like to revise that opinion,' Marc said with a grin as he stepped outside the motor-caravan.

A group of about twenty people were waiting out-side for them. Marc recognised some of them from the village. They were carrying banners calling for the cancellation of the rock concert. Of Miss Rumford there was no sign, which Marc thought was strange. He would have thought that she would be right at the very front of the group she supported so enthusiastically.

Scott sighed and then smiled half-heartedly at the

protest group. 'Good evening,' he said pleasantly enough. 'What can I do for you?'

'You must call off the concert,' said a middle-aged man, who Marc recognised as Bert Wilkins, the landlord of the local pub.

'You all know I can't do that,' Scott said reasonably. 'It's all arranged. The local police have given their permission.'

'There'll be evil at the concert.' This came from Miss Stebbins, the village postmistress.

Scott smiled indulgently. 'I can assure you that there'll be professional security on site at all times,' he promised them.

The protesters weren't buying any of that. Trouble-makers and villains would be turning up at the concert they told Scott, people they didn't want in their village. Despite all of Scott's assurances, it soon seemed that things were about to turn nasty.

'I don't understand,' Marc whispered to Scott. 'The people down in Brentmouth are usually quite a placid lot. I've never seen them this angry before.'

'Something's happened to annoy them,' Scott guessed.

'Or someone,' Marc realised and pointed to the back of the crowd. The twins were standing there, their weird green eyes glaring at them.

'Who're the blond-haired guys?'

'Two prize creeps, that's who,' Marc said. 'It seems they're not happy with upsetting things just at the Institute. Looks like they want to cause trouble in the village as well.'

Sure enough, one of the twins spoke up. 'Don't listen to their lies,' he told the assembled villagers. 'The Zarathustra concert is going to bring trouble to your village.'

'That's right,' the other twin said. 'There's already been an increase in burglaries since their kind came to town. Imagine what will happen when hundreds of thousands of rock fans come here.'

There was a murmur of anger among the crowd. The recent burglaries had been worrying most of them and they certainly didn't want any similar trouble descending on their normally sleepy village.

'Thieves and vandals, drug-dealers and drunk-ards,' the twins chorused as one. 'Do you want scum like that to come to your village?'

'No,' was the villagers' unanimous response.

'Then drive them out of your home!' one of the twins said. He picked up a stone from the ground and flung it at Marc and Scott. It hit Marc on the shoulder.

'Let's get out of here,' Marc said, as another stone was thrown at them. This one struck the side of Scott's motor-caravan. The older man was already racing to the driver's seat at the front of the vehicle. Another stone caught Marc on the hand and blood started to flow.

'Drive them out of here!' the twins said, as the villagers started to follow their lead and throw stones at Marc and Scott. 'Don't let their kind and their devil's music poison your green and pleasant lands!'

The villagers had been whipped up into a frenzy now and they advanced menacingly on the van as

Scott tried desperately to turn the engine. Finally it started and the van rumbled off down the Rise and to safety, with the villagers jeering and shaking their fists after it.

The twins smiled at each other, knowing that their plan was working. The concert would go ahead, they both realised that. After all, what were a handful of discontented villagers compared to thousands of rock fans who had been waiting for the gig for years?

But feeling was running high now in the village, just as it was up at the Institute. It was those feelings, those *minds*, that mattered.

And in the Darkfell Ring the stones glowed once again, and the Demons that lived there licked their lips in anticipation of the coming feast.

Seven thousand years ago, those who had lived near the Darkfell Rise had been too primitive, their minds gristle when the Demons had demanded meat. Now things had changed. Now the Demons would feast indeed!

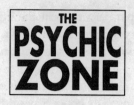

THE PSYCHIC ZONE

12

Under Arrest

Dateline: The Institute;
Friday 26 June; 08.25.

'So where were you last night?' Marc asked Rebecca when they met up by the lockers before the start of classes. 'I came round to show you something really wild.'

'Up at Fetch Hill watching the comet, where else?' Rebecca said. She looked curiously at the small bag which Marc was taking out of his locker. 'What's that?'

'What I wanted to show you,' he said. 'Something which will even drag you from your radio telescope. Something Miss Rumford gave me.'

Rebecca sighed and raised her eyes heavenwards. 'Her broomstick maybe?' she cracked. 'Something the fairies left her?'

'Better than that,' Marc replied with a grin. 'How are you on spectrographic analysis?'

Marc was about to open the bag when Eva came marching down the corridor. He hastily replaced the bag back inside his locker, and shut and locked the door.

Eva looked the two of them up and down with the sort of superior stare which she normally reserved for street beggars, manual labourers and pushy parents. She made a great show of looking at her watch: a gold Rolex. Not for the first time Marc and Rebecca wondered how a mere school secretary could afford such expensive belongings.

'I think it is time for class now, *ja*?' she said.

'Er, yes, Eva,' Marc said and looked nervously back at his locker. Had Eva seen him put the bag in there?

'Not for you, Mr Price,' Eva said. 'You are to report to General Axford's office.'

'Axford's back?' asked Marc. If Miss Rumford heard this she'd be round here like a shot, asking him for his help in stopping tomorrow's concert. Eva shook her head.

'Sergeant Sadler wishes to speak to you in the General's office,' she told him, and when Marc and Rebecca looked blank, she added: 'he has been called in because of the unfortunate incident last night.'

'Unfortunate incident?' asked Rebecca. 'What do you mean?'

Behind her dark glasses, Eva raised a supercilious eyebrow. It was clear that she wasn't going to tell her. Instead, she took Marc by the arm – her grip was firm, and Marc winced at her touch – and marched him down the corridor towards the General's office.

As Rebecca watched them go, Joey walked through the main doors and came up to her. He grinned.

'Marc in trouble again with his slipping grades?' he asked as he walked over to his own locker which was covered with Zarathustra stickers. He unlocked and opened the door and took out several text books.

'No, the police,' Rebecca said. She stroked her chin thoughtfully. Marc wasn't exactly the best-behaved of all her friends but as far as she knew he'd never been in trouble with the law before.

'I saw a whole squad of cop cars pass by the Institute last night, heading for the village,' Joey told her.

'Maybe they're something to do with the concert?'

'Nah. Scott – that's the guy who's organising the gig – is handling his own security,' Joey informed her.

'Does he think that there's going to be trouble?' Rebecca asked.

Joey shrugged his shoulders. 'Maybe,' he said, 'if there's a repeat of what happened last night. He near as well got lynched by the locals. Marc came by my room and told me about it, before he went out looking for you. He'd cut his hand and he needed to clean it up.'

'Maybe that's what this Sadler guy wants to talk to him about,' Rebecca wondered.

Dateline: The Institute, General Axford's Office; Friday 26 June; 08.45.

Sergeant Sadler was as different from Digby Ashby as it was possible to imagine. Tall and gaunt, he had a cruel and mean face, and his eyes glinted coldly when Eva escorted Marc into the office. Eva led Marc to a chair, where he sat down, and she hovered in the background, listening in on the conversation.

'You are Marc Price?' he asked.

Marc nodded. 'What's this all about, sir?' he asked.

'And you knew Miss Olive Rumford?'

Marc frowned. 'That's right,' he said. *Knew*? What did he mean, *knew*?

'And you were with her yesterday, Mr Price?'

Marc nodded once more. 'I was at her home yesterday afternoon. Where is all this leading to, sir?' he wanted to know.

'Miss Rumford has gone missing from Rowan Cottage,' Sadler informed him steelily. 'She was due to meet some friends to organise a last-minute protest against the rock concert.'

'And she didn't turn up?'

Sadler nodded. 'One of them became worried and called round to her cottage,' he continued. 'But, of course, you would know that, wouldn't you, Mr Price?'

Marc suddenly had a very bad feeling about Sergeant Sadler's questioning. 'What do you mean, sir?'

'The place was completely wrecked,' he told him.

'Another of these burglaries, then,' Marc guessed.

'Miss Rumford must have put up quite a struggle,' Sergeant Sadler continued. 'There was blood all over the walls and the doors.'

'I don't understand,' Marc said.

Sadler looked meaningfully down at the cut on Marc's hand, and Marc suddenly realised what he was thinking.

'Come on,' he said nervously, 'you surely don't think that I had anything to do with this.'

'Where were you yesterday evening?' Sadler demanded.

'I went round to Rebecca Storm's – she's a friend of mine. She lives a couple of miles away from the Institute with her mother.'

'And she can back up your story?'

'No. She wasn't in,' Marc replied. 'Her mother's away and Rebecca was up at Fetch Hill.'

'So you have no evidence to show that you weren't at Rowan Cottage yesterday evening.'

Marc fixed the sergeant with a defiant stare. 'And neither do you have any evidence to prove that I was.'

Sadler sat back in his chair and smiled a contented smile. 'But we do,' he told him, and glanced over to Eva. Eva walked to the door and opened it.

Colette walked nervously into the room. She was still wearing her dark glasses and, as she approached the sergeant, she glanced guiltily at Marc.

'Is this the person you saw leaving Rowan Cottage last night?' Sadler asked.

Colette nodded. 'That's right. I was taking a short-cut home, when I saw him,' she said. 'He seemed to be in quite a rush.'

Marc stared wide-eyed at his friend. 'Colette, why are you lying?' he asked in amazement. 'You know I wasn't at Rowan Cottage last night. It must have been burglars. Maybe they were looking for –'

He stopped himself just in time, as he remembered Miss Rumford's earlier words: *they've been breaking into houses, searching for the Lodestone.*

Colette looked sadly at Marc and shook her head. 'I'm sorry, Marc,' she said, 'I have to tell them the truth. You were at Rowan Cottage last night. I wasn't mistaken. I saw you there.'

Sergeant Sadler stood up and came around the desk. He placed a heavy hand on Marc's shoulder. 'Marc Price, I wonder if you would accompany me to the station. I'd like you to help us with our enquiries concerning the abduction and possible murder of Olive Elizabeth Rumford.'

Helping us with our enquiries. Marc knew exactly what that meant.

'But I didn't do it,' Marc protested as Sadler bustled him out of the office, followed by Eva and Colette.

'That'll be for others to decide,' Sadler said, and then added with relish: 'looks like you're going to miss your precious rock concert after all, doesn't it?'

Dateline: The Institute;
Friday 26 June; 10.15.

'What was I supposed to do?' Colette asked tearfully, after Marc had been led away and she had been confronted by Rebecca and Joey on the green outside the school's main building. 'I couldn't lie to the policeman, could I?'

'Are you sure it was Marc you saw outside Rowan Cottage last night?' Rebecca asked.

'Of course I am,' Colette said. She walked over to a bench and sat down, ramming her hands into the pockets of her jeans.

Joey looked suspiciously at Colette. 'And what were you doing there at that time of the night?' he asked.

'Taking a short-cut home, like I told the police,' Colette replied and returned Joey's accusing stare. 'You don't believe me, do you?'

'We just think you might have been mistaken, that's all,' Rebecca said as diplomatically as she could.

Joey, however, wasn't so diplomatic. 'You've been acting strangely lately,' he told her. 'Mixing with the wrong crowd.'

'You mean the twins?' Colette asked.

'You said it – not me,' Joey replied.

'Why don't you trust them, instead of trying to see the bad in everyone?' Colette asked. 'They're really nice people once you get to know them. It was their idea to ask that Scott guy at the concert to arrange free entry for all the Institute kids.'

'It was?'

'Of course,' Colette said and smiled smugly. 'Which just proves that you're wrong.'

'But when we saw you by the Darkfell Ring, we thought that they were bullying you –'

'Which shows just how wrong you can be – even if you are studying at the Institute. We were having a bit of fun, that's all. They're not the heartless bullies you think they are.'

Rebecca sighed. She knew that Colette always had a tendency to see good in people, even when it was patently obvious that they didn't deserve her trust.

'Why would Marc break into Miss Rumford's cottage?' Colette asked Rebecca, careful to avoid Joey's probing eyes. 'Whatever could he find there which would be interesting?'

'He told me that he'd found something –' Rebecca began, and was surprised by Colette's sudden reaction. Colette grabbed hold of her hand.

'Yes?' she asked. 'What is it that he found?'

Rebecca looked strangely at Colette, and was about to answer her when Joey interrupted.

'It was that old book on fairies she promised him, right?' he said cheerily. 'You know, sometimes I think our Marc is turning out to be a prize jerk!'

Colette relaxed again and her sudden enthusiasm dimmed. She glanced at her watch. 'I have to go now,' she told them. 'I promised I'd meet the twins at ten-thirty.'

'You'll have to hurry then,' Rebecca said.

'I'll get there,' Colette said confidently and walked

off down the path. When she was out of earshot, Joey turned to Rebecca.

'Beam me up, Scotty,' he said.

'What?'

'Never mind.'

'What was all that about the book?' Rebecca asked him. 'Why didn't you want Colette to know what Marc had found?'

'Colette's not acting normally,' Joey said.

'Sure, she's mixing with a couple of creeps, and she's suddenly taken a liking for Zarathustra albums,' Rebecca said. 'But apart from that, she seems to be fine.'

'I think she's lying about Marc,' Joey said.

'Why should she?' Rebecca needed to know. 'What possible purpose could that serve?'

Joey shrugged his shoulders. 'Who knows?' he asked. 'But you know how I've always been able to sense Colette's presence before?'

'Sure, sometimes it gives me the creeps,' Rebecca admitted, 'the way you always seem to know where she is, or how she's feeling.'

'We've a mild psychic link, that's all,' Joey said nonchalantly as though it were the most natural thing in the world. 'But when I was looking at Colette then, there was nothing. You know how it is when you look at yourself in the mirror? Your reflection appears flat, and, even though it moves when you move, you know it's not the real you. That's how I felt when I was looking at Colette just now.'

'And what was with all that "beam me up, Scotty"

stuff?' Rebecca asked, but Joey just grinned.

'So what *is* it that Marc found at Miss Rumford's?' he asked. Rebecca led him back into the school building and to the row of lockers in the corridor.

'He locked it away before I could see it,' she said. 'I guess we won't know until the police set him free.'

'Oh yes we will,' Joey said. He looked around to make sure that no one was looking, and then took from out of his pockets what looked to Rebecca like a length of intricately twisted wire.

'The Institute might be one of the top schools in the country but there are some things that you can only learn back home in Harlem,' Joey grinned and inserted the wire into the lock of Marc's locker. A few twists and turns, and the door sprang open.

'I'm impressed,' Rebecca said, as she took out the small bag that Marc had placed there.

'The NYPD weren't,' Joey remembered with a smile. He watched on as Rebecca took the Lodestone from out of the bag. 'What is it?'

'Search me,' Rebecca said and handed it over to Joey. He turned it over in his hands and examined the design on its face. 'This remind you of something?' he asked her.

Rebecca frowned. There was something vaguely familiar about the design but she couldn't quite put her finger on it. 'You tell me,' she said.

'Remember when we went to the Darkfell Ring?' Joey reminded her. 'This is the same design we saw on the altar stone.'

Rebecca took the Lodestone back from Joey. 'That's

impossible,' she said. 'What possible connection could this have with the Darkfell Ring?'

She examined the design again: several dots connected by lines. They reminded her of something – but it wasn't the inscription on the stones of the Darkfell Ring.

Finally she realised what it was. She should have seen it straight away, but this was hardly the sort of thing you'd expect to find on a seven-thousand-year-old lump of rock.

'Scorpio!' she said. 'It's the constellation of Scorpio – the constellation that Comet Zarathustra is passing through right now!'

Dateline: Brentmouth Police Station;
Friday 26 June; 15.15.

Marc stared disconsolately at the walls of the interview room in Brentmouth Police Station. At least they hadn't thrown him in a cell, he thought miserably, although this was probably just as bad. Paint peeled on the mouldy walls, and the cup of tea a kindly WPC had given him lay cold and untouched on the rickety desk.

He'd asked to make a telephone call, but Sergeant Sadler had told him that that was strictly out of the question (which it wasn't, Marc knew). He'd even questioned the policeman's right to bring him to the station at all. Colette's evidence would hardly stand up in a court of law.

'I've been here for almost six hours now,' he told Sadler. 'Are you going to press charges, or do the sensible thing and let me go?'

'You'll find out soon enough,' Sadler grunted. 'There's someone coming up from London to see you.'

'From London?' Marc asked and wondered who it might be.

Had General Axford perhaps heard of his dilemma from Eva, and come up from the city to vouch for his innocence and character? Marc dismissed that thought from his mind almost instantly. Eva was probably taking the greatest delight in imagining him locked up in Brentmouth Police Station.

He was soon given his answer. The door to the interview room opened, and in walked a tall, military-looking figure wearing dark glasses. Marc recognised him instantly as John Smith, the man who had come up to investigate the missing aircraft. Smith nodded a curt hello to Sadler and then dismissed the junior man.

'So you're the boy who Sadler thinks is responsible for Olive Rumford's disappearance,' he said, and casually tossed a file down on to the desk. Marc recognised the crest on the cover: the Ministry of Defence.

'I didn't do it,' Marc protested his innocence once again. He was surprised to see Smith smile.

'Did I say you did?' Smith said. 'I instructed Sadler to warn me if any strange disappearances occurred in Brentmouth.'

'Sadler's working for you,' Marc realised. 'That's why you had Ashby transferred down to London.'

'Maybe,' Smith said. 'Or perhaps I just wanted the Zarathustra concert to go ahead.'

Marc looked strangely at John Smith. He didn't seem the sort of man who'd enjoy a Zarathustra gig. But then neither did Colette.

'You were the last person to see Olive alive, is that right?'

Marc nodded. 'Alive? Do you think she's dead?'

John Smith shrugged his shoulders. 'Dead or alive, it doesn't really matter to me,' he said coldly. 'When you saw her, was she worried about anything?'

'She was concerned about the burglaries that have been happening around here,' he remembered. 'And about the Darkfell Ring . . .'

'The Darkfell Ring?'

'That ring of stones up on the Rise,' Marc replied, and then looked defiantly at Smith. 'I'd've thought that you would have known about that if you work for the Government.'

'Did I say I did?' Smith asked mysteriously, and smiled to himself. 'So tell me what Olive told you about this Darkfell Ring.'

'She said it had something to do with all the disappearances over the years – like her fiancé – and the aircraft that went down here a few weeks ago,' Marc said.

'Olive always had her little flights of fancy,' Smith recalled. 'She liked to think that she was a witch, of course. Believed in fairies too, or so I hear.'

'You knew her?' Marc asked. Smith seemed to be very familiar with Olive Rumford's background.

'Knew *of* her,' Smith corrected him. 'We have files on anyone who's been connected in any way with the disappearances. Including you.'

'Me?'

'And your friends Rebecca and Joey. You saw the plane crash – even though you claimed you didn't.'

Marc looked at the file in front of Smith and at the Ministry of Defence crest on its cover. If Smith was indeed working for the MoD, then he bet it was a very special part of it. Could he be working for the mysterious Project?

'That's why you called General Axford down to London, so you could ask him questions about us?' Marc asked.

'That's right,' John Smith replied. He leant forward so that he could look Marc straight in the eyes. Even through the older man's dark glasses Marc could still feel the force of his personality.

'You're not hiding anything from me, are you?' he demanded. Marc discovered that he needed all his willpower not to tell the man the truth.

'Of – of course not,' he lied.

'Because if you are, then you could find yourself in very deep trouble,' Smith threatened him. 'Very deep trouble indeed.'

Marc forced himself to return Smith's steely stare. 'Can I go now?' he asked.

Smith smiled his most insincere smile. 'Of course, you can,' he said. 'After all, you're not under arrest, are you?'

'That's not what Sadler led me to believe,' Marc pointed out.

'When I heard about your involvement with Olive's disappearance –'

'I was not involved!'

'I needed to make things clear to you. I asked Sadler to bring you in to me. It seems that he took me a little too literally.'

'Yeah, I'm sure,' Marc said. 'With a little help from Colette too.'

'Colette?'

'Yeah, you got her to lie and say that I was round Miss Rumford's house last night.'

John Smith shook his head. According to him he knew nothing about anyone called Colette. Still, he made a note in his file all the same.

'Stay out of things you don't understand, Marc,' Smith warned him, and, as Marc stood up to go, he added: 'and one more thing – enjoy the concert tomorrow night!'

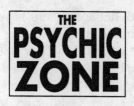

THE PSYCHIC ZONE

13

Memories Set in Stone

*Dateline: The Institute, Study Bedroom 331B;
Friday 26 June; 22.15.*

'Colette, get out of here, OK?'

Colette's face fell. She was standing in the open doorway to Marc's study bedroom at the Institute. Marc had opened the door for her when she'd knocked but he hadn't invited her in.

'I said I'm sorry,' Colette said.

'You nearly got me arrested,' Marc said, 'with your lies about seeing me at Rowan Cottage last night.'

'I was mistaken, but I really did think that it was you,' Colette said. 'And I couldn't lie to the police sergeant.'

Rebecca looked at Marc. 'Be easy on her, Marc,' she said softly.

'No way,' he said grumpily, even though he was beginning to feel a little guilty about his harsh manner with Colette. 'All her accusations have done is to stir up bad feeling in the village.'

'Bad feeling?' asked Joey, who was sitting on Marc's bed, holding the bag which contained the Lodestone.

'Yeah, some of the villagers are saying that it's an Institute student who's abducted Miss Rumford,' Marc told them all. 'The Institute isn't exactly popular with some of the locals who think we're just a bunch of stuck-up know-it-alls. This is all we need.'

'You can't blame Colette for that,' Rebecca pointed out reasonably.

'Her accusations haven't exactly helped though, have they?' Marc pointed out bitterly.

Joey let out a long whistle of appreciation. 'Wow, when I came to the Institute I thought Brentmouth was a sleepy little village. I never reckoned on major rock concerts, protest groups, and the locals accusing us kids of kidnapping and murder!'

Colette tried one last time. 'I'm sorry, Marc,' she said. 'Maybe I should go into the village and explain things?'

'Yeah, maybe you should,' Marc said sullenly.

For what seemed the first time Colette noticed the bag on Joey's lap. She asked him what it was.

'It's none of your business, Colette!' Marc said angrily. 'Now get out of here. Go with your new friends.'

'The twins are down in the village,' she told him. 'And I wish you'd find it in yourself to like them.'

That was the last straw, and Marc shut the door in Colette's face. He turned back to Rebecca and Joey.

'You were too harsh on her,' Rebecca said.

'Maybe I was,' Marc said and asked Joey to take the Lodestone out of its bag. 'I didn't want that Smith guy to find out about this.'

'Who do you think he is?' Rebecca asked.

'I don't know, but I bet you he's not one of the good guys,' Marc said. 'Maybe he's from the Project. Maybe he's – Look at the Lodestone!'

Cradled in Joey's hand, the Lodestone was faintly glowing. The lines joining the stars of Scorpio were twinkling and flickering in the light from Marc's desk lamp. As the three of them watched on, the light slowly faded, and then went out.

'It can't be,' Rebecca gasped. 'A lump of stone can't pulse with light like that.'

'Now do you believe me?' Marc asked with satisfaction. He took the stone from Joey and placed it in the centre of his desk. 'OK, Joey, do your stuff.'

'What's he doing?' Rebecca asked as she watched Joey pick up the Lodestone and press it to his forehead.

'A simple experiment in psychometry,' Marc explained.

'What?'

'Learning the history of an object through touching it.'

'That's impossible.'

'So are stones that glow in the dark. Now sssh, Joey needs complete quiet for this. If he's disturbed it could be fatal for him . . .'

CHANGELINGS

Dateline: The Darkfell Rise;
5000BC.

Joey relaxed his grip on his own mind, melding his thoughts with the Lodestone which was pressed against his forehead, burning into his imagination. He was seeing what it had seen down through the centuries. He was learning its history. Hundreds of thousands of sounds chittered in his head, and he knew that those were the voices of the Demons of the Darkfell Ring.

He seemed to be falling down a long, long tunnel of stars. At the end of the star-tunnel there was a small blue object, spinning in the darkness. He knew what it was. He recognised it from NASA photographs.

It was the Earth. A younger, cleaner Earth, barely touched yet by mankind.

Something else came into view: a wooded hill. He knew that this was the Darkfell Rise. Long before its trees had been chopped down way back in the Seventeenth century. Long before mankind had built the Darkfell Ring.

There was a horrible thudding noise and suddenly everything went black. For a few seconds Joey found it difficult to breathe. He panicked.

And then the lights came on. Green, eerie lights. He looked around him. He seemed to be in some sort of small chamber. Six bodies lay in what looked like six stone honeycombs. He couldn't see them very clearly, for they were swathed in some sort of green mist. But he had the feeling that, whoever these creatures were, they were very, very weak – maybe even dying.

Joey's mind sped forwards through the centuries. He was now standing in the middle of the Darkfell Ring. Trees towered high all around the six stones, but within the circle the soil was barren.

He heard laughter. He looked to see where it was coming from. Two people were approaching him. They couldn't see him of course, so he took his time to study them.

A boy and a girl, a couple of years older than him. Walking hand in hand. There was something strange about them, and it took Joey a couple of seconds to realise what it was.

It was their clothes, which were made out of some coarse material. The boy's hair was long. The girl's hair was braided. Neither of them looked as though they'd had a wash in weeks.

The boy pressed the girl against one of the Darkfell stones and started to kiss her passionately. The girl responded with equal passion.

Joey was about to turn away, when the strangest thing happened. Two of the creatures he had seen in the honeycombs appeared in the centre of the circle. They approached the two lovers, who were standing frozen with fear. Green mist seemed to appear out of nowhere. The stones of the Darkfell Ring were glowing now.

'God's blood!' he heard the boy say, as one of the

creatures reached out a long-fingered hand towards him. 'What manner of spirit is this?'

And then the creature somehow changed, taking on the appearance of the boy he had touched. The boy turned pale and collapsed to the ground, and Joey watched on in horror as his body faded from sight. The young girl screamed as the second creature approached her.

Joey shut his eyes. He didn't want to see any more.

When he opened them again, he was still standing in the Darkfell Ring, but now no trees towered around it. He saw an old woman standing by the Needle Stone. She was carrying something in her hand.

And then his mind moved on again. This time he was back in the stone chamber. Five of the stone honeycombs were occupied – but not by the creatures.

He inspected the first one. Colette was lying there, in some sort of coma, her eyes wide-open and unseeing. He was about to look into the next honeycomb when –

Dateline: The Institute, Study Bedroom 331B;
Friday 26 June; 22.27.

– the door to Marc's room burst open, and the twins and Colette were standing there. There was a greedy look in the twins' green eyes as they advanced towards Marc, Rebecca and Joey. Joey was in a daze, slumped by Marc's desk and his concentration broken by the twins' sudden entrance. The hand holding the Lodestone was hanging down by his side.

'Get away from here!' Marc cried out as Colette moved towards Joey. The Lodestone was glowing in his hand, pulsing with its unearthly light.

'We must have the Lodestone!' Romulus said. His green snake-eyes now seemed to be glowing as brightly as the Lodestone itself. There was evil in those eyes. There was greed in them as well.

'It is ours by right!' added Remus. He licked his lips. His tongue seemed almost lizard-like. Marc was reminded of his chameleons back in the biology lab.

Colette darted forward and snatched at the stone amulet in Joey's hand. Joey was so dazed that he was unable to put up any resistance. Colette could easily have grabbed it from him, if it hadn't been for Rebecca. She hit out at the younger girl, knocking her to the ground. Colette's dark glasses fell off, and she snarled at Rebecca. Beneath those glasses, her eyes – normally blue and timid – were now green and staring, as green and staring as the twins' own eyes.

'What have you done to Colette!' Rebecca demanded.

'She's one of us now,' the twins said in unison as they slowly approached Marc and Rebecca. 'She will join us in the Feeding Time.'

Joey had now regained consciousness, and he looked at the twins and Colette. Perhaps it had something to do with the shock of his being woken out of his trance, but he seemed to be seeing them for the first time. And what he saw filled him with horror.

'That's not Colette,' he said with certainty. 'And you're not the twins.'

The twins laughed and Colette joined in. 'Who else could we be, Joey?' Colette asked.

'I don't know, but I do know that you don't belong here, not here, not in Brentmouth, not at the Institute, not – not –' Joey paused, and the twins sneered at him.

'Not belong where?' they asked, grinning.

'You don't belong on this planet,' Joey realised. His hand clasped the Lodestone even more tightly, something which Romulus and Remus couldn't fail to notice.

'Give us the Lodestone!' they snarled. 'It was taken away from us all those years ago. It belongs to us and to no one else.'

Joey remembered the vision he had of the old woman in the Darkfell Ring. She had been Olive Rumford's ancestress, he realised, and it had been she who had taken the Lodestone in the first place. It had been she who had passed it down through the generations. And it had been for the Lodestone that Olive Rumford had been murdered.

The twins lunged at Joey and knocked him to the ground. They reached for the Lodestone, which was glowing more brightly than it had ever done before. Rebecca rushed forward and tried to pull them off Joey, but Colette dragged her back.

'The Lodestone! The Time of Feeding is at hand. We must have it!' the twins cried. Now they made no attempt to disguise their voices. The sound that came

from their lips was dark and rasping – and unmist-
akably alien.

The attentions of the twins and Colette had been so
fixed on the Lodestone in Joey's hand that they had
all ignored Marc. Now Marc seized his chance. He
glanced over at Joey, and Joey knew what Marc had
on his mind.

The twins were on top of Joey now, trying to wrest
the Lodestone from his hand. With one almighty effort
Joey pushed them off and threw the Lodestone over
to Marc. The twins watched as the stone – now glowing with an almost blinding light – arced over their
heads and into Marc's outstretched hand.

'Run, Marc!' Joey cried, as the twins and Colette
turned on Marc.

Marc didn't need any encouragement. He raced for
the open door and ran out into the corridor, slamming
the door shut behind him. The twins and Colette
started to follow him, but Joey and Rebecca grabbed
hold of them, delaying their pursuit. With an angry
roar, Colette and the twins threw them off and headed
after Marc.

By the time they'd opened the door and poured
out into the corridor, Marc had already disappeared.
They looked this way and that, and the twins' nostrils
flared, as if trying to scent out their human quarry
like hounds on the hunt of the helpless fox.

Seconds later, Rebecca and Joey raced out of the
room, determined to stop the twins and Colette from
following Marc.

And then they stopped in their tracks. The corridor

was empty. There was no sign whatsoever of the twins and the creature that was pretending to be Colette.

'That's impossible,' Rebecca said, as she looked down the corridor towards the closed lift doors. The lift was still on their floor; the twins and Colette obviously hadn't taken that route in their pursuit of Marc. 'They can't have just vanished into thin air.'

Joey nodded his head wisely. 'Beam me up, Scotty,' he said, with an ironic grin.

THE PSYCHIC ZONE

14

Why Aren't You Dead?

Dateline: The Darkfell Rise;
Friday 26 June; 23.03.

Marc stumbled up and over the bumps and mounds of the Darkfell Rise. He wasn't quite sure where he was making for. He didn't know why he was heading in this direction. All he knew was that he had to escape from the twins and Colette. He had to prevent them from getting their hands on the Lodestone – whatever the Lodestone was. And whatever the twins and Colette really were.

The Lodestone was still glowing, but not quite as brightly as it had done back in his room at the Institute. However, it now seemed to be pulsing with a regular rhythm. If Marc had spent any time with Rebecca at the Fetch Hill Radio Telescope he would have recognised it as precisely the same signal which was being given out by Comet Zarathustra.

The wind was becoming wilder and ever wilder now around the Darkfell Rise. It lashed Marc's face; it made his eyes water. A strange whining sound seemed to fill the air – the sound of all the Demons of the Darkfell Rise, reaching out for the Lodestone.

Before Marc there stood the stones of the Darkfell Ring. They were glowing once again, pulsing in time with the Lodestone in his hand. Marc started to race towards the six stones, as if he thought that he could find some sort of sanctuary there.

And then he stopped. There was no safety there, within the Ring, he realised. The stones were drawing him to themselves, like a magnet draws iron to itself, or like a spider welcomes a fly into its web. Just as the Darkfell Ring had attracted others to itself down the ages. Just as it had captured the missing villagers over the centuries. Just as it had spirited away the three passengers of that aircraft which he, Rebecca and Joey had seen crash-land.

And there, waiting for him, inside the Darkfell Ring, were three figures – the twins and Colette. Their eyes were blazing with green fire. Their tongues were licking their lips. Their hands were outstretched, urging him to them.

Marc was so frightened that he didn't even think how they could have reached the Darkfell Ring before him. In his hand the Lodestone glowed brightly.

'Come to us, Marc,' Colette intoned. 'Bring us back the Lodestone. Join us in the Feeding Time.'

But Marc knew now that it wasn't Colette speaking.

Someone – some*thing* – had taken over her body and appearance. Something deadly. Something evil. Something alien.

He turned to run. For a second, Colette made to follow him, and then the twins held her back.

The lights of the Institute were too far away now. It had taken Marc a good half-hour or so to reach here. But, just a little way off in the distance, he could see another set of lights – the lights from Scott Masters' motor-caravan. He ran off in that direction.

Within a little less than five minutes Marc had reached Scott's caravan. Why wasn't he being followed, he should have asked himself. But he was far too frightened to think straight. In his hand the Lodestone still glowed with a fast-fading light.

He banged on the door of Scott's caravan for what seemed like hours but was little more than a few seconds. Finally the door opened and Scott peered out. He was wearing a dressing gown, and he rubbed his brilliantly-blue eyes and focused on Marc.

'What's up?' he asked and attempted a joke: 'the gig's tomorrow, not tonight, you know!'

'Scott, you have to let me in,' Marc said and pushed past him into the caravan. He threw himself down on to the ramshackle sofa there, throwing on to the floor Scott's copy of *Cosmological Review*.

'What's wrong?' Scott asked and saw for the first time the Lodestone in Marc's hand. 'And what's that?'

'I don't know,' Marc admitted. In the background he could hear the sound of one of Zarathustra's greatest hits. The light from the Lodestone dimmed and then went out. Scott reached over and turned off his radio. 'But whatever it is, they want it.'

'Who wants it?' Scott asked.

'The twins,' Marc said. 'Their eyes – they're like the Devil's own.' He looked up into Scott's eyes. They were blue and piercing, so different to the twins' eyes.

'Those two blond-haired creeps who tried to halt tomorrow's gig?' Scott asked.

'That's right,' Marc said and then stopped. Hadn't Colette said that it had been the twins who had persuaded Scott to give all the Institute students free admission to the gig? Before he could query Scott on that matter, the older man had reopened the door and taken a look outside.

'There's no one there now,' he told him. 'But I've just seen the weirdest thing. Those stones up on the Darkfell Ring. I could swear that they're glowing . . .'

'Glowing?' Marc looked down at the Lodestone. It was dull and grey now, and no longer shining with that weird, unearthly light.

'Is that what they were after?' asked Scott.

'Yes,' Marc said and showed it to Scott. He handed it over to him so that Scott could look at it more closely.

'What is it?' Scott asked. 'Some sort of lucky charm?'

Marc shrugged his shoulders. He had no idea, he admitted, but pointed out to him the plan of Scorpio on the Lodestone's face.

'You think it has something to do with this comet?'

'Search me.'

Scott thought for a moment. 'Look, why don't I look after this for you?' he suggested. 'For safekeeping.'

Marc wasn't so sure. 'What's to stop the twins trying to steal it from you?' he asked him.

Scott went over and opened the door of the caravan again. 'Do you see them out there?' he said, reasonably enough. 'There's no one out there on the Rise. You've obviously lost them. Let me keep the Lodestone and then it'll be safe – at least until after the gig tomorrow.'

Marc considered the matter. He guessed that Scott was probably right. If the twins and whatever it was that looked like Colette had known where he was then they would have tracked him down by now. And how could they suspect that the Lodestone was now in Scott's possession?

He nodded his head. Yes, he agreed, Scott could keep the Lodestone for the time being. At least the twins wouldn't think of looking for it here. And in the meantime he'd have the opportunity to find out just what was so special about the stone.

'So go back to Rebecca and Joey and don't worry about anything,' Scott said. 'Believe me, after tomorrow's gig, all this won't matter at all.'

And, as Marc left Scott's motor-caravan and headed off down the hill back towards the Institute, he wondered about Scott's last remark: *after tomorrow's gig, all this won't matter at all*. What had he meant?

Dateline: The Institute, Study Bedroom 331B;
Saturday 27 June; 01.13.

Marc finally reached his study bedroom back at the Institute and was surprised to find that Rebecca and Joey were still waiting for him there. He affected a look of dismay.

'Gee, thanks, guys,' he said sarcastically. 'I might have thought that you'd have come after me and tried to help me.'

Rebecca and Joey exchanged worried looks and then glanced behind them at the other person in the room, whom Marc hadn't seen. General John Smith strode forwards, looking even more sinister than usual in his slick black suit and dark glasses. Marc took a step back, knowing that behind those glasses Smith's eyes would surely blaze with the same unnatural light as the twins' and Colette's.

'How did you get in here?' Marc wanted to know. 'What do you want?'

'You're hiding something from me, boy,' Smith said. 'And I told you not to do that. Now where is it?'

'Where's what?' Marc feigned ignorance. He threw a look at Rebecca and Joey. Had they told Smith anything about the Lodestone? They both shook their heads. Smith had learnt nothing from them.

'Our detectors picked up an unusual amount of electromagnetic radiation coming from the Institute,' Smith said.

'*Our* detectors?' Marc asked. 'Who are "we"?'

'That is classified information,' came Smith's infuriating reply.

'Your gizmos probably got their wires crossed,' Joey said flippantly. 'They probably picked up something from the radio telescope up on Fetch Hill.'

Rebecca shook her head. 'Fetch Hill is closed for the night,' she told him. 'And all day tomorrow. The big boys down in London are monitoring the comet now that Prof Henderson and the others have all been given free tickets for the Zarathustra gig.'

'Just like us at the Institute,' Joey said. 'Although what Scott thinks we and the Fetch Hill crew have in common is beyond me.'

Smith ignored Joey and took another step towards Marc. 'We can make you talk, boy,' he said menacingly. 'We can make you tell us what it is you're hiding from us.'

And then it suddenly dawned on Marc. John Smith was even more in the dark than he, Rebecca and Joey were. He didn't know about the Lodestone. All he knew was that an unusual amount of radioactivity had been detected coming from this area. He thought about the way the Lodestone and the Darkfell Ring had glowed. Was that what John Smith's detectors had tracked down?

'Is that a threat?' he asked.

'Yes,' came back the response.

'You can't hurt Marc,' Rebeca said.

'Don't you be too sure of that,' Joey muttered.

'I can have him arrested for the murder of Olive Rumford,' Smith said.

'Come off it,' Marc scoffed and took another step back. If he could just make a run for it . . . 'You've no evidence.'

'I don't need evidence,' Smith said.

'Evidence? Good gracious, evidence of what?'

Everyone turned to look at the newcomer who was walking down the corridor, in the opposite direction to which Marc had looked. Olive Rumford smiled at them all and peered at them through heavy-rimmed glasses, different to her normal pair of spectacles.

'Miss Rumford! Why aren't you dead?' Joey said, rather tactlessly.

'Dead? I can assure you that I most certainly am not!'

'Your glasses – what happened to them?' Rebecca asked warily.

'I broke them in a fall at the cottage. I'm wearing these until I can replace them.'

Joey turned to John Smith with a triumphant smile on his face. 'Tough luck, General,' he said cheekily. 'It's gonna be pretty difficult to arrest Marc for a murder when the corpse is still alive and kicking!'

Smith looked at Marc, then Miss Rumford, and then back at Marc again. Recognising that he had been thwarted, at least for now, he stormed out of Marc's study bedroom.

'Who was that unpleasant young man?' Miss Rumford asked.

'He's called John Smith,' said Joey, 'and if he isn't one of the baddies then I'm Michael Jackson.'

'And what was he doing here?'

'Who knows?' Rebecca asked and shrugged her shoulders. 'Maybe he wanted to get his hands on your family heirloom . . .'

Miss Rumford looked curiously at Rebecca through her new dark glasses. 'What do you mean?'

'Marc told us both about the Lode –' Rebecca began, but Marc stopped her.

'What are you doing here at the Institute, Miss Rumford?' he asked suspiciously. 'I thought you'd be busy at Rowan Cottage, organising the opposition to the Zarathustra gig.'

'Opposition?' Miss Rumford asked. 'The very thought of it! I was passing by the Institute and the night porter let me in. I wanted to check that you were all going to the concert tomorrow.'

'Sure we are,' Joey said.

'You can count me out,' Rebecca put in.

'Then I shall see you all there!' said Miss Rumford, the woman who had protested the loudest against the gig. 'And you know something – I can't wait!'

THE PSYCHIC ZONE

15

The Demons of the Darkfell Ring

Dateline: The Darkfell Rise;
Saturday 27 June; 09.10.

'I must be crazy coming here with you two,' Rebecca said the following morning as she, Marc and Joey trudged up the Darkfell Rise towards the stage area. 'I don't even like the blasted band.'

'Hey, you'll change your mind when you hear them,' Joey said brightly. 'Just look at Miss Rumford.'

'That's what's worrying me,' Marc said thoughtfully. 'Why is the Zarathustra gig so important to her?'

'We agreed to worry about that after the concert this afternoon,' Joey said and looked at Rebecca. 'Any news of Colette?'

Rebecca shook her head. 'I rang up Miss Kerr. Colette didn't come home last night,' she told them. 'I think we should tell the police.'

'Tell them what?' Marc asked reasonably enough. 'That one of our mates has been possessed by two creepy, green-eyed bullies who're interested in a lump of stone that glows in the dark? Sadler would laugh at us and pack us all off to the local loony bin!'

'If John Smith doesn't get to us first,' Joey said. 'Those dark glasses of his give me the major creeps. He's involved with all this somehow.'

'We still don't know exactly what "all this" is,' Rebecca pointed out.

'Maybe not, but it's all centred around the stones,' Marc said and looked over to the Darkfell Ring. Scott's motor-caravan was still parked nearby.

'And the comet,' Rebecca said. She looked in the opposite direction, towards Fetch Hill. 'Today it'll be the closest that it's been to Earth for seven thousand years.'

By now they had reached the main stage area. A section directly in front of the stage had been cordoned off, and security guards were patrolling the perimeter. When they saw Marc, Rebecca and Joey approaching they made to move them away.

'It's OK, guys,' said a familiar voice. 'They're students from the Institute. They all get in free and get to be the nearest to Zarathustra.'

Scott came forward to join them, and Marc introduced Rebecca to him. Rebecca thought that she had never seen anyone with eyes so brilliantly blue. Scott shook her hand.

'So you're the girl who thinks that Zarathustra are a bunch of talentless forty-somethings?' he said, and Rebecca shot Marc an angry look.

'Not guilty,' he said. 'I didn't tell him!'

'Then how did you know?' Rebecca was about to ask, when Scott pointed to the computer console at the front of the stage.

'Do you think that you can handle that, Joey?' he asked.

Joey rubbed his hands with glee. 'You bet!' he said.

'That controls the sound systems,' Scott said and indicated the two towering speakers on either side of the stage.

'That's certainly some serious hardware,' Rebecca said. 'I've never seen sound systems like that before.'

'It's the very best,' he agreed.

'Can I have a closer look at it?'

'Later,' Scott said quickly. He turned to Marc. 'You ready for your job, Marc?'

Marc, Scott told them, was to help out with security. His job was to identify Institute students and usher them into the part of the Rise exclusively reserved for them. Rebecca started to giggle.

'Marc Price – a bouncer,' she said. 'That's a bit like a seven-stone weakling thinking he can take on Mike Tyson.'

'Thank you very much – I don't think,' Marc said. 'It'll give me the greatest of pleasure turning away some of those drongos from Year Six.'

Suddenly they heard the unmistakable sound of helicopter blades cutting through the sky. They all looked and shaded their eyes as a large, brightly-coloured 'copter came into view. A cheer went up from the crowds who were even now congregating on the Darkfell Rise.

'Zarathustra!' Joey exclaimed, turning around and giving Scott a hearty pat on the back. 'Congratulations, Scotty, my man. You really have done it. You've finally got the biggest band in rock back together again.'

Rebecca pointed to the crowds, who were waving to the helicopter as it started its descent to the VIP area at the rear of the stage. 'Look at them,' she said, genuinely impressed in spite of herself. 'They're beside themselves with excitement. It's as if it's the second coming.'

Scott smiled secretly to himself. 'Yes, it is, isn't it?' he said. He stood watching the cheering crowds for a few more moments and then addressed Marc. 'You ready, Marc?'

'In a few minutes, OK, Scott?' Marc said. In the distance he could see the twins sauntering over up the hill towards them. He had no wish to talk to them just now. 'There's something I want to take a look at first.'

'The Lodestone's safe, if that's what you're worried about,' Scott said.

'I'm not worried,' Marc lied, and walked off in the direction of the Darkfell Ring.

Dateline: The Darkfell Rise;
Saturday 27 June; 09.33.

There was no doubt about it, Marc decided as he approached the six standing stones. The Darkfell Ring was glowing. This wasn't the bright June sunshine catching mica deposits, as Rebecca had suggested. This wasn't a trick of the light, or the product of his over-active imagination.

No, the stones of the Darkfell Ring were blazing with their own eerie light. But this time the light seemed different somehow. Stronger, brighter, much more constant.

Marc had noticed it as soon as the helicopter had flown in and the crowds had cheered the arrival of their rock heroes. It was as if their outpouring of emotion – strong, unchecked emotion – had somehow caused the stones to shine.

And then he remembered how the stones had glowed when the twins had been caught bullying Peter Lee. Strong, unchecked emotion – but that time fear, not joy.

And then he thought of how the Lodestone had shone when he had been attacked by the twins and 'Colette'. Fear again, and excitement. Strong, unchecked emotion.

And Joey had told him of his vision of the two young lovers. Strong, unchecked emotion, once more; that time passion and love.

And blazing the fiercest of all were the altar stone

and the Needle's Eye. Marc walked up to the Needle Stone, crossing over the soil that had been barren since before anyone could remember.

He peered through the Needle's Eye, looking to the north. He saw the Institute buildings. He saw the Fetch Hill Radio Telescope, its dish and antenna also pointing northwards. Pointing towards the Comet Zarathustra. It couldn't be a coincidence.

Could it?

Marc then looked at the large altar stone, the stone on which some said sacrifices were made to the sun god in ancient times. He passed his hand over the strange symbols which had been etched on to the stone.

Green mists started to swirl around Marc. He began to feel woozy. The world started to spin sickeningly around him. He was beginning to find it hard to breathe.

For several frightening moments everything went black. When Marc came to, he found himself lying on the floor of the stone chamber which Joey had described to him. The first thing he saw was the stone slab on the ceiling. He recognised it as the underside of the altar stone. Seeing the carvings from this side – the side they were originally meant to be viewed from – he recognised them instantly. The constellation of Scorpio. And then the path of Comet Zarathustra, as he had seen it in Rebecca's copy of *Cosmological Review*.

He knew where he was!

He was underneath the Darkfell Ring; how deep he couldn't tell, for he had no way of knowing how thick the altar slab above him was. And he finally knew what the Darkfell Ring was.

When they had all first visited the Ring, Rebecca had said that the configuration of the stones had reminded her of something: an equilateral triangle. A small stump at its apex: that was all that remained of the cockpit. Two slanted stones at the other two angles: they were the wing-tips.

The Darkfell Ring was all that could be seen of a stone spacecraft, a spacecraft that had crash-landed here almost seven thousand years ago! A stone spacecraft buried in the earth of the Darkfell Rise, that earth in which nothing would grow.

Just as Joey had done before him, Marc looked round the interior of the spacecraft. He was in a small circular space, which he immediately thought of as the cabin. It was little more than four metres in diameter. The stone walls – if they really were stone, and they very probably weren't – shone with a ghostly phosphorescent light which pulsated at regular intervals. If Marc had ever accompanied Rebecca to the Fetch Hill Radio Telescope, he would have recognised it as the same pattern which was coming from the Zarathustra Comet.

Marc walked up to the honeycomb nearest to him and peered inside. He stepped back in shock. Lying within the honeycomb was one of the twins, eyes wide open and staring straight ahead. There was something different about the twin, and it took Marc a few seconds to understand what it was. This twin's eyes were blue, not green. He looked into the adjoining honeycomb. Sure enough, the twin's brother was lying there in the same open-eyed coma.

So if these were the twins, who were the people Marc had seen heading off for the Zarathustra concert, the very same people who had started a reign of bullying and terror back at the Institute?

He looked into the next honeycomb. Olive Rumford. But he had seen Olive Rumford only yesterday night, hadn't he?

No, he'd seen someone who only looked like Olive Rumford. The Olive Rumford he knew had hated the prospect of a rock band like Zarathustra invading the Darkfell Ring. Yet the Olive Rumford of last night couldn't wait for the gig to take place.

Just like Colette, he realised. Colette had never been able to stand Zarathustra's music. And there she was, probably up on the Darkfell Rise now along with the twins, eagerly awaiting the concert.

What was so important about the Zarathustra gig? What was so important about the reappearance of a band which no one had seen for years? What was so important about a band everyone was so crazy for that no one had talked about anything else for months?

And then Marc realised exactly what it was. It was the same thing which had made the stones of the Darkfell Ring glow. It was what had made the Lodestone shine when he and Rebecca had lost their temper with each other.

Strong, unchecked emotions.

The strong, unchecked emotions of the thousands of Zarathustra fans. The strong, unchecked emotions of the kids who had been bullied by the twins. The strong, unchecked emotions of the villagers during their protests. Even his own uneasiness and fear when he thought that he was being arrested for Olive Rumford's murder. He bet that the Darkfell stones had glowed then as well.

And then he looked at the fourth honeycomb. He might have guessed it. Colette was lying there – the real Colette, captured by the Demons of the Darkfell Ring, her eyes timid and blue, rather than evil and green as he had last seen them when she'd invaded his room.

Marc reached out and touched her: her body was cold. He tried to shake her awake. She murmured a little in her deep sleep, but, apart from that, didn't respond to his touch.

And then Marc looked into the fifth of the six honeycombs, and his heart skipped a beat. He recognised the figure in there as well. Seth Murray, Miss Rumford's fiancé from all those years ago. Still as young as he looked in that newspaper photo he'd been shown. And yes, Miss Rumford had been right. He was the very spitting image of Scott Masters – except for one thing.

Whereas Scott's eyes had been blue, Seth's were green, and Marc suddenly knew why green had always been known in folklore as the colour of evil. Now he realised why some called the shade 'the fairies' colour'.

The twins at the Institute, the new, more confident Colette who sided with bullies, the Miss Rumford who loved rock music: they were all changelings, their bodies copied and hijacked by the Demons of the Darkfell Ring.

'You know, don't you?'

Marc spun around. The twins were standing there. He turned back to look at the other, real, twins in the honeycomb.

'You're right,' one of the green-eyed twins said. 'We stole their bodies when they were flying in towards the Institute.'

'But how did you snatch them from the plane?' Marc spluttered, and took a step backwards as the twins approached him. For the first time he saw that the tongues which licked their lips greedily were forked, just like those of the chameleons in his own lab back at the Institute.

'How did we get here so quickly when you saw us only minutes ago?' Romulus asked and walked menacingly towards Marc.

'How did Colette manage to leave you and the Williams child and be with Rebecca at Fetch Hill only moments later?' asked Remus. 'How did Colette bring Olive Rumford away from Rowan Cottage and within the Darkfell Ring?'

'How have people always vanished within the Darkfell Ring over the centuries, while we have waited patiently?'

'I don't understand,' Marc said, although in his heart of hearts he knew exactly what the evil green-eyed twins were talking about.

'Beam me up, Scotty,' the twins sneered. 'We

transport away their bodies and keep them here. Without their genetic code to study we could never assume their images. We could never convince your people that we are as they are.'

'You're not human,' Marc realised with a strange mixture of fear and elation. 'You're . . . you're aliens. Body-snatching aliens!'

Remus grinned his evil, superior grin. 'Aliens who taught men the secret of fire,' he boasted. 'Who, for over seven thousand years have shown your miserable species how to survive. How to think. How to reason. How to build weapons of destruction and unlock the great secrets of the universe.'

'Until we approach the Feeding Time,' Romulus chuckled. 'Until humanity is so advanced that hundreds of the finest minds in the world, the greatest brains, the fiercest intelligences –'

'Intelligences that we ourselves have influenced down the years,' Remus said. 'We have never been lazy, no matter what bodies we assumed at the time –'

'Until those intelligences are gathered together, excited by one common bond,' Romulus said. 'Strong, unchecked emotions.'

'The Zarathustra concert,' Marc realised. 'No matter who you are, everyone on the planet possesses strong feelings about the group. It's going to be the biggest media event in the world.'

'And those strong feelings we shall use,' Remus said. 'That is why it is so good that the man Scott Masters has ensured that all the Institute students attend the concert.'

'Scott doesn't realise that by organising the Zarathustra concert he's helping you,' Marc said. 'Wait a minute – you said, "the fiercest intelligences". You're using our minds, the minds of all the kids at the Institute!'

'Exactly, Marc Price, and to ensure our own survival,' Romulus said. 'And, if mankind should die in the process, then what is that to the Demons of the Darkfell Ring?'

'Our planet is dead and dying,' Remus continued, 'weakened by constant centuries of war.'

'Then more fool you,' Marc countered. 'At least down here on the Earth we're finally coming to our senses.'

'And our species is almost worn out and extinct, crippled by radiation sickness,' Romulus added. 'That is why we are searching the galaxy for new life.'

'To feed on like vampires,' Marc realised and looked back at the bodies of Colette and of Olive Rumford and Seth Murray and the two real twins.

'To adopt their bodies so that we may continue our own lives. Seven thousand years ago our main craft sent us down here to seek new intelligences which we could feed on.'

Seven thousand years. Marc thought back to what Rebecca had told him. *Seven thousand years since the comet Zarathustra had last visited Earth.*

'The comet is your spacecraft!' he suddenly realised.

'Now returning for the Feeding Time,' Romulus said and licked his lips. 'All those minds from the

Institute, excited and agitated by the Zarathustra concert, soaked up by the stones of the Darkfell Ring. Enough food there for our race to survive for another seven thousand years. Enough bodies there to feed on till your tiny planet is just another burnt cinder floating around in space.'

'You can't do that,' Marc protested.

'Aha, but we are, even now,' Remus said. 'All we need is to channel power from our returning mothership and the feasting can begin.'

'A channel?' Marc asked. 'But you'd need some sort of focus for that . . .'

'And soon we shall have it, Marc Price, soon we shall have our hands on the Lodestone. In just a few hours' time our ship will be at its closest point to Earth. It will send out its contact beam. And we, the Raath, will feed again, taking over all those new bodies.'

And it was then that Marc Price started to feel very scared indeed.

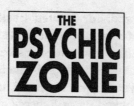

THE PSYCHIC ZONE

16

Feeding Time

Dateline: The Darkfell Rise;
Saturday 27 June; 13.10.

Rebecca Storm grimaced and looked northwards to the Fetch Hill Radio Telescope. That was where she wanted to be now, and not at some second-rate pop concert. In just over an hour's time Zarathustra would be at its closest to Earth. But with Prof Henderson having locked up the complex for the day, there was nothing else for her to do but have her eardrums blasted out by some of the lousiest music she'd heard in ages.

She pushed her way through the crowd of Institute students who were thronging the VIP area, head-banging along to the music from the support band: a bunch of eighties has-beens called The Lower Depths. Their heavy-metal music was whipping up the crowd into a frenzy and, for heaven's sake, Zarathustra hadn't even put in an appearance yet.

Joey was by the computer console at the front of the stage, checking the sound levels on the ultra-modern PA system which Scott had brought in especially. He looked up as Rebecca approached.

'Isn't this great?' he asked.

'Yeah, sure,' Rebecca said, with a tone which clearly suggested that she was lying. 'Have you seen Marc?'

Joey shook his head. 'Scott's been looking all over the place for him,' he told her. 'If he doesn't hurry he's going to miss the main event.' He looked up at the sound system. 'Have you ever seen muthas like those before?' he asked, and Rebecca shook her head.

'I'd like to take a look at them when the gig's over,' she said.

'You staying then?'

'I'm going to look for Marc first,' she said. 'He went off in the direction of the Ring, didn't he?'

'That's right,' Joey replied.

Suddenly there was an enormous cheer from the crowd as The Lower Depths finished their set and Scott Masters walked on to the stage. This was the man who had brought Zarathustra together, they knew; this was the man who was directly responsible for the concert. As far as they were concerned, he was a hero.

'And now, the moment you've been waiting for for years,' Scott announced to the expectant crowd. 'Ladies, and gentlemen! Students from the Institute! I give you the one and only Zarathustra!'

The applause was deafening as the four members of Zarathustra, one of the greatest bands ever in the history of rock, walked on to the stage and launched into their first number.

Rebecca groaned.

'I'm outta here,' she said to a disbelieving Joey, who was already bopping away to the music.

As Rebecca pushed her way through the crowds, she wasn't aware that she was being followed. Looking out of place in his black suit and dark glasses, John Smith made his way to the Darkfell Ring.

Dateline: The Darkfell Ring;
Saturday 27 June; 13.22.

Marc looked in despair at his surroundings. The twins had left hours ago now, disappearing into thin air and leaving him alone. He had tried to wake Colette and the others, but they hadn't responded to his words and repeated shakings.

Even underground he could dimly hear the music of Zarathustra and the cheers of the crowds. Soon they would be in such a state of excitement that the twins – or the Raath, as they had described themselves – would be able to feed on their minds, taking over their bodies just as they had done with the real twins.

The twins had told him that they had been stealing bodies for millenia now, not just on this planet but on others dotted about in this sector of the Milky Way.

The original humans were kept down here in their spacecraft, for without their continued existence the Raath would soon revert to their original appearance and die soon thereafter.

He looked up at the altar stone slab. If only he could get out and warn Scott and the others. For if he didn't and the twins found the Lodestone, then all hell would break loose on the Darkfell Rise.

But how? There seemed to be no opening mechanism. Indeed, there seemed to be very little recognisable technology on board the small craft. But who knew what alien technology looked like?

Strong, unchecked emotion! Of course that was it, Marc realised. That was what all the technology of the Raath was based on. In their case it had been hate and aggression and fear. But there were other emotions too. Love, compassion, friendship.

Marc stood underneath the altar slab and closed his eyes. He thought of Rebecca and Joey and Colette. He couldn't let them down. They'd stood by him in bad times – Rebecca had even swallowed her principles once and given him the answers to a physics exam when his grades had been slipping. Now it was his turn to repay.

He thought gratefully of his parents, who had sacrificed much to top up his scholarship at the Institute. He even thought of some of his teachers back at the Institute. He thought of Olive Rumford and the love she had had for Seth.

And then he thought of the thousands out there even now on the Darkfell Rise. He had to do it for them. He couldn't let the Raath take over their bodies and feed on them, like vampires sucking out their existence.

Slowly, green mists started to swirl around Marc . . .

Dateline: The Darkfell Ring;
Saturday 27 June; 13.25.

Even by the Darkfell Ring the sound of cheering was so loud that it almost drowned out Zarathustra's music. Rebecca wondered what the crowds saw in them, as she trudged up the Rise looking for Marc.

And then she stopped and gasped. The stones of the Darkfell Ring were glowing, glowing as they had never done before. It was impossible, she knew, but she had to believe the evidence of her own eyes. And as the noise from the crowd became louder and louder, so the light from the stones became brighter and brighter.

'Interesting, isn't it? Unnatural even. *Alien.*'

Rebecca spun around. John Smith was standing before her. He had sneaked up on her silently. His cruel mouth smiled at her and the sun glinted off his dark glasses.

Rebecca took a step back. She watched on in horror as Smith took a gun from out of his jacket. Was he going to kill her?

'I saw them too, that's why I came here as well,' he told her, but made no attempt to come any nearer. 'It's part of what has been picked by our detectors.'

'Who are you?' she asked, but, before John Smith could answer, several things happened at once.

There was an enormous cheer from the crowds, as Zarathustra launched into one of their greatest hits. The stones were now glowing with an eerie brilliance.

Scott Masters came running up the hill clutching something in his hand, and John Smith raised the gun to fire at him.

And then a pillar of green mist appeared in the exact centre of the Darkfell Ring, and from out of it staggered Marc.

Marc took in everything at once. He saw John Smith with the revolver, and mistakenly thought that he was going to fire at Rebecca. He raced forwards, head down, and headbutted the older man in the stomach. Smith fell to the ground, and the gun went flying out of his hand and landed in the grass.

As he hit the ground, Smith's dark glasses were knocked off, and Marc looked at the man's face, expecting to see the glowing green eyes of the Raath.

John Smith's eyes were bright blue.

Rebecca came up to Marc and directed his attention to Scott. The rock promoter seemed to be oblivious to what was going on around him. Instead, he walked – almost reverentially – into the Darkfell Ring and stood before the Needle Stone. In his hand he was carrying the Lodestone.

'Scott! No!' Marc called out, as he watched the young man place the Lodestone in the empty Needle's

Eye, the place Olive Rumford's ancestress had taken it from all those years ago.

'What's happening?' Rebecca asked.

'I've got a really bad feeling about this,' Marc said.

They watched on as the light from the Needle's Eye grew so bright that they had to shade their eyes to protect them from its brilliance.

And then from out of the sky burst a beam of light and focused on the Needle's Eye. Rebecca watched on as a second beam of light shot out of the Needle Stone and connected with the antenna of the Fetch Hill Radio Telescope.

'At last, the Feast is about to begin!' Scott said and laughed.

'You can't be the Raath!' Marc protested.

Scott turned to Marc and seemed to notice him for the first time. There was a superior look in his blue eyes. It wasn't a particularly pleasant look.

'Can't I?' Scott said and sneered. And then, to Marc's horror, he reached up and took the blue contact lenses from out of his eyes. There blazed the green eyes of the Raath.

'What are you?' Rebecca asked. 'What have you done to the Fetch Hill Radio Telescope?'

'The Lodestone is old and weakened,' Scott told them. 'With its power linked up to the radio telescope, its might is increased triplefold to contact our brethren in space.'

'But how could you operate the –' Rebecca began and then realised. 'Colette. When she came to collect that magazine?'

'She altered the angle of the antenna, bringing it

perfectly in line with Zarathustra and opening a channel for the Raath to feed on,' Scott explained. 'It was necessary too. We did not then know that we would find the Lodestone in time. The radio telescope provided a suitable substitute.'

In all the excitement, everyone had forgotten about John Smith. He crawled through the grass and reached out for the revolver which Marc had knocked out of his hand. He took aim and fired – not at Scott but at the Lodestone in the Needle's Eye. The stone shattered into a thousand pieces.

But still the stones of the Darkfell Ring carried on glowing.

'Your futile attempt was in vain,' Scott said. 'Now contact has been made through Fetch Hill we no longer need the Lodestone.' He laughed. 'Nothing can stop the Raath now – nothing and no one in the world.'

Then the mists descended on the creature called Scott Masters, and when Marc, Rebecca and Smith had blinked, he had disappeared.

'We have to evacuate the area,' Smith said, reaching into his pocket for his mobile phone and starting to race off down the hill. 'I can get my men on to it.'

'It's going to be too late,' Marc said. 'Nothing can stop them now.'

Rebecca looked thoughtfully at the Needle Stone and then back at the Fetch Hill Radio Telescope. She clapped her hands for joy. 'Oh yes there is!' she said. 'Come on, we have to get Joey!'

Dateline: The Darkfell Ring;
Saturday 27 June; 14.14.

Zarathustra were still playing when Marc, Rebecca and Smith got back to the stage area, but there was something strange about the audience. They were no longer cheering or dancing along to the music. Instead, they were staggering about, as if they were drunk, their eyes glazed over, as if they were drugged.

On stage, the band seemed oblivious to what was going on. Maybe they'd all been hypnotised by the power of the Raath as well, Rebecca thought. She looked at Marc and Smith. That same glazed look was in their eyes now, too. Only she was immune to the power of the Raath. Only she had not been whipped up into a frenzy by the prospect of Zarathustra playing!

She pushed her way through the crowd of near-zombies, and headed for the front of the stage. Joey was there, his head slumped over the computer console which regulated the two speakers on either side of the stage.

Only they weren't speakers at all, Rebecca now realised. They were devices of the Raath, designed to feed off the crowd's fevered emotions, just as the Darkfell stones absorbed their psychic energies. Frantically she jabbed at the 'off' switch.

Nothing happened.

'Damn!' she cursed. She pushed the switch again.

Still nothing happened.

There was nothing for it but to drag the semi-conscious Joey away from the console. He put up no resistance as she led him through the crowds, past the still-stunned Marc and Smith, and out of the concert area. She lay him down on the grass.

'Joey? Joey? Can you hear me?' she cried. She slapped him across the face.

'Hey! What was that for?' Joey asked and opened his eyes groggily. He could still just hear Zarathustra playing. 'I've got to get back to the gig. Those guys are – say, what happened?'

'Never mind, Joey,' Rebecca said urgently. 'We have to get to Fetch Hill. Now'

'Look, can't this wait until after the gig –'

'This is important,' Rebecca said.' Are there any cars around here?'

'There's Scott's motor-caravan,' Joey said. 'He's not using it at the moment. Say, aren't you too young to drive?'

'Sure I am,' Rebecca said. 'But if we don't get to Fetch Hill in time, then there'll never be another gig for any of us ever again!'

Dateline: Fetch Hill Radio Telescope;
Saturday 27 June; 16.11.

'Come on, Joey! Hurry up!' Rebecca said impatiently, and looked behind her. The corridor leading up to the telescope control room of Fetch Hill was empty, but she knew that Scott and the twins could appear at any moment. If they realised what she was trying to do then they wouldn't hesitate to kill her and Joey.

Joey looked up. He was crouched down on the floor by the locked door of the control room, inserting his piece of twisted wire into the lock.

'Look, it's been a while since I did any proper breaking and entering, you know,' he said grumpily. 'Opening the main door was a mutha of a thing to do. It wasn't like breaking into Marc's locker.'

'I know, but we have to hurry.' She looked at her watch. Comet Zarathustra would be at its closest to Earth in exactly four minutes' time.

Finally there came a click – probably the most eagerly awaited click in Rebecca's life – and the door sprang open. Rebecca rushed into the room, with Joey hot on her heels. She looked up at the digital clock on the wall. 16.12: three minutes to go.

Rebecca raced over to the command bank which controlled most of the major functions of the radio telescope. If she could just work out what Colette had done, she might still be able to stop the Raath taking over the bodies of the concert-goers.

16.13.

'I wouldn't do that, my dear,' came a familiar voice from behind her. Olive Rumford was standing there, green eyes blazing greedily. She reached out and attempted to pull Rebecca away from the controls. Rebecca jabbed her elbow backwards, trying to push her away.

More arms reached out for Rebecca. Colette was by

her side now, wresting her arms away from the levers and switches before her.

'You must not stop the Feeding!' she rasped. 'The Raath must survive! We may not be able to stand another hibernation within the Darkfell Ring.'

16.14

'We are weak,' said Scott, who had now appeared before her in a shroud of green mist. 'We leave the Darkfell Ring only when we need to feed off the mental energies of others. The rest of the time we sleep.'

'But when we have the energies of the Zarathustra concert then we shall be strong again!' said Colette and licked her lips greedily.

That was Colette's fatal mistake, reminding Rebecca of the danger all of them were facing. Rebecca turned back to the controls.

On the digital clock the seconds counted down towards 16.15.

Thirty seconds . . .

'Stop her!' The twins had now appeared from no-where and they reached out for Rebecca's arms, successfully dragging them away from the console.

Twenty-five seconds . . .

Joey leapt on to the back of one of the twins and pulled him off Rebecca. He kicked the other in the shins.

Twenty seconds . . .

With aching fingers Rebecca reached out for the controls. If she could just alter the angle of the radio telescope by just one degree, even half a degree.

Fifteen seconds . . .

'We cannot wait another seven thousand years!' Scott growled.

Ten seconds . . .

'The Feasting must be now,' Miss Rumford said.

Five seconds . . .

Rebecca stretched out further. The others tried to pull her back.

Four . . .

Just an inch more . . .

Three . . .

Rebecca's hand touched the switch, and pulled down hard.

Two . . .

From above them all they could hear a tinny scrunching sound – the sound of the metal dish of the radio telescope altering its angle.

One!

16.15.

The five Raath stood before Rebecca. It was as though they had shed their skin. Now she was seeing them as they really were. The Demons of the Darkfell Ring, thin and emaciated, their green eyes glaring evilly at her.

'Zarathustra is gone,' the Raath that had been Olive Rumford said.

'It shall never come again,' 'Scott' moaned.

'Not for seven thousand years,' said the Colette-Raath.

'The Earth girl has defeated us,' the twins said as one.

Rebecca stood back. She was sure that the Raath would kill her now. Joey steeled himself for action, ready to spring to Rebecca's defence.

And then the green mists descended, and when they looked again the Raath were gone.

But before they went, was it Rebecca's imagination, or did she hear what sounded like a sigh?

THE PSYCHIC ZONE

17

Suspicions

*Dateline: Brentmouth Cottage Hospital;
Friday 3 July; 11.14.*

'Well, I feel a little sorry for them.'

Rebecca, Marc and Joey looked on in amazement at Colette. It had been a week since the Zarathustra concert and Colette was recuperating well from her ordeal. She was sitting up in her hospital bed now, and taking solids again, which was a good sign.

'Are you out of your tree, Colette?' Joey asked. 'They took over your body.'

'We should have noticed sooner,' Marc said. 'Your friendship with the twins. Your interest in science. The way you could get from the Darkfell Ring to Fetch Hill in a matter of minutes.'

'Why are you sorry for them, Colette?' Rebecca asked.

'All they wanted to do was to survive,' she said. 'Who's to say we wouldn't have done the same thing in the same situation?'

Marc sighed. It was good to have the old Colette back, always finding good in everyone.

'Well, it's over now,' Marc said, 'and we all have Rebecca to thank.'

'It was only because I hated Zarathustra's music that I wasn't affected and could think on my feet,' she said. 'I realised that if we could alter the angle of the Fetch Hill antenna we could stop the Raath sending their signal.'

'But they managed to send a signal to the Lodestone before it was destroyed,' Colette said.

'We still had plenty of time,' Rebecca said smugly. 'Radio waves travel much more slowly than light waves.'

'I don't call one second "plenty of time",' Joey complained.

Just then the door opened. John Smith walked in.

'Are you feeling better?' he asked Colette.

'The odd nightmare or two, but that's all.'

'You'll have to be fully debriefed of course, just like the others. Miss Rumford is proving to be a particularly awkward one to convince.'

Marc smiled. That sounded like the Miss Rumford he knew. 'It's going to be difficult coming to terms with Seth being much younger than her.'

'Green-eyed Seth, too,' Rebecca said with a grin. '*Natural* green eyes – not the green of the Raath.'

'What will happen to the Raath?' asked Colette.

'When we broke into the Darkfell Ring they were very weak,' he informed them crisply. 'The psychic forces generated by the concert were their last hope of survival. They all died within a matter of hours. Once the psychic link with their human templates was broken, they all regained full consciousness.'

Marc glared at Smith. Even though they had misjudged him, he still didn't like the man. He wondered if he was telling the truth, or whether the five Raath had been taken to some Government laboratory somewhere and dissected. If Smith did work for the Government at all, that was.

'You never did tell us exactly who you work for,' Joey said.

'No, I didn't, did I?' Smith said and smiled. 'But we'll be keeping a watch on you kids from now on. Just remember – this thing didn't happen at all, OK?'

And with that, Smith marched out of the room. But somehow they all knew that they'd see him again sometime.

'Can you believe the nerve of that creep?' Joey asked, but Colette was more concerned with Rebecca.

'What's wrong? You look worried.'

Rebecca stroked her chin. 'This all started with the three missing passengers,' she said.

'That's right,' said Marc who couldn't quite see what Rebecca was meaning.

'Two of them – the real twins – were taken over by the Raath,' she said. 'So what happened to the pilot?'

They all exchanged a puzzled look. None of them had ever thought of that before.

'Hang on a minute, when I went into the spacecraft, there were six honeycombs there,' Marc said, and Joey nodded.

'And only five were occupied,' he said.

'What are you trying to say?' asked Colette. 'That there might be another Raath somewhere, one who survived?'

'It's possible, isn't it?' Rebecca said. 'Maybe even more.'

The door opened once again and Eva walked in. She looked at Rebecca, Marc and Joey, and it was plain from the expression on her face that she didn't like what she saw.

'I gave you three permission to miss your first lessons this morning to visit your friend,' she said and looked at her expensive Rolex watch. 'I see you are abusing that privilege. You will all return to the Institute at once, *ja*?'

Marc, Rebecca and Joey all sighed and followed Eva out of the room. It looked as though this meant an end to their adventures for a while.

And as Eva led the way out, the July sunshine glinted brightly on her dark glasses.

BOOK 1
MINDFIRE

Mathew Stone

The Institute is a school for brilliant young scientists, but even Marc, Rebecca, Joey and Colette can't explain away some weird and sinister events . . .

A ball of flames sets part of the Institute on fire, but this is no accident. For clearly burnt into the ground is the eerie outline of a fox. Could this be anything to do with an ancient curse laid on the old Abbey – where the Institute now stands . . ?

Paranormal? Or a cover up? The truth lies in the psychic zone . . .

BOOK 3
ALIEN SEA

Mathew Stone

The Institute is a school for brilliant young scientists, but even Marc, Rebecca, Joey and Colette can't explain away some weird and sinister events . . .

The gang's holiday in Cornwall is interrupted by the discovery of a micro-circuit by a group of archeogists digging for ancient relics of King Arthur. And now one of the diggers is having nightmares! But when the gang ask questions, they're threatened by some nasty thugs. *Who* wants this discovery kept a secret?

Paranormal? Or a cover up? The truth lies in the psychic zone . . .

THE PSYCHIC ZONE

ORDER FORM

0 340 69836 5	MINDFIRE	£3.99 ☐
0 340 69840 3	CHANGELINGS	£3.99 ☐
0 340 69841 1	ALIEN SEA	£3.99 ☐

All Hodder Children's books are available at your local bookshop or newsagent, or can be ordered direct from the publisher. Just tick the titles you want and fill in the form below. Prices and availability subject to change without notice.

Hodder Children's Books, Cash Sales Department, Bookpoint, 39 Milton Park, Abingdon, OXON, OX14 4TD, UK. If you have a credit card you may order by telephone – 01235 831700.

Please enclose a cheque or postal order made payable to Bookpoint Ltd to the value of the cover price and allow the following for postage and packing:
UK & BFPO – £1.00 for the first book, 50p for the second book, and 30p for each additional book ordered up to a maximum charge of £3.00.
OVERSEAS & EIRE – £2.00 for the first book, £1.00 for the second book, and 50p for each additional book.

Name ....

Address ....

....

....

If you would prefer to pay by credit card, please complete:
Please debit my Visa/Access/Diner's Card/American Express (delete as applicable) card no:

Signature ....

Expiry Date ....